BEAUTY
AND
BEASTLY

STEAMPUNK BEAUTY AND THE BEAST
MELANIE KARSAK

Beauty and Beastly: Steampunk Beauty and the Beast
Steampunk Fairy Tales

Clockpunk Press, 2017

Published by Clockpunk Press
Cover design by Karri Klawiter
Editing by Becky Stephens Editing
Proofreading by Siren Editing
Proofreading by Rare Bird Editing

In loving memory of Edward and Margaret Kernick

With love to Dana
xox

Melanie Kernick

THIS BOOK BELONGS TO:

_____

BEAUTY

AND

BEASTLY

1
BONJOUR

"ISABELLE, ARE YOU COMING?"

My heels clicking on the cobblestone, I hurried behind Papa as I made the last few notes in my journal. The London streets were packed. A group of young airship jockeys, each jostling the other around, bumped into me as they passed. My fountain pen went skidding across the page, blotting ink on my sketch.

"Blast," I cursed, glaring.

"So sorry, miss," a young airship captain said. "Are you headed to the market? May I buy you a new journal?"

I frowned at him, suddenly wondering if it had been an accident.

"No. No, thank you," I said. I slipped my pen into its holder hidden amongst the flowers and feathers on my tiny lady's top hat and tucked my book into my basket. Grabbing the skirt of my blue gown, I hurried to catch up to Papa as he made his way through the massive arch at the entrance of the Hungerford Market.

I found my father reading over his shopping list and dodging oncoming shoppers as we entered the busy market.

"Know what you're after?" he asked distractedly as he ran his finger down his list.

"Yes, Papa. The trick is not finding too many things."

He chuckled. "Indeed. Indeed. At Hungerford Market, that is always a problem. I'm headed to Tinker's Hall. You?"

"Mister Denick first. I need some new reading materials for the trip. I'll join you in the hall afterward. Keep an eye out for a glass cylinder for me? Two centimeters or so in length, smallest in circumference that you see?"

"Of course," Papa said, pinching my cheek.

The market was bustling. Everywhere I looked I saw mechanics, tinkers, chemists, and airship crews. Aside from them were common folk hunting consumables and textiles. I gazed down the aisles. On this end of the market were the fish-mongers, fruit and flower vendors, and butchers. On the far end of the market was Tinker's Hall. While the hall sold all manner of wares for someone in our trade, it was also part social club for the London Tinkers Society, of which Papa was a leading member. No doubt he would be lost for an hour or more hobnobbing with his peers. Waving to Papa, I turned and headed in the other direction to Antiquarians' Hall where Mister Denick kept his bookshop.

But first...

"Good morning, Isabelle," the baker called when he saw me. He was holding out a freshly-baked egg custard tart wrapped in parchment.

I had to smile. Had I become so predictable? I suppose every Wednesday morning was the same as the Wednesday morning the week before. Papa and I left our workshop along the Thames at precisely eight thirty. We arrived at the Hunger-ford Market at 9:15. Papa always went to Tinker's Hall. I always went to Mister Denick's bookstore, stopping at the baker's stall first for an egg custard tart. I'd peruse his wares, but like always, he had the same old things, and I bought the same tart. Every Wednesday it was the same routine. It was 9:17, and I was there for my egg custard.

"Thank you, sir," I said, pressing a coin into his hand in exchange. "Good day."

"And to you."

As I walked, I munched the tiny confection. The sweet taste of the buttery crust. The egg custard baked with a firm surface but soft, smooth, filling. The tart still warm from the baker's oven. Perfection. This was why I never tried anything new. Why change what worked?

"Hello, Isabelle," Miss Ting called from her stall.

I waved to her. "Good morning, Miss Ting."

"Need silk string today?" she asked.

I shook my head. "All stocked up!"

She waved happily.

"Isabelle the beauty," Mister White called then waved. The tobacco vendor, a massive pipe hanging from his mouth, was all smiles.

I nodded politely then waved. Mister White was still under the impression that I should let his son woo me. I had decided it wasn't my place to inform him that his son had eyes for Master Johnson's apprentice, Tom. I turned the corner to Antiquarian's Hall.

Here, the place was less crowded. Well-dressed ladies and gentlemen perused fine artwork from early masters, estate furniture in need of a home, and other beautiful goods from years past.

As I passed two well-dressed women, one of them whispered to her companion. They both looked at me then started giggling.

I looked down at my dress only to see that my bodice was utterly covered in crumbles. When I went to wipe the custard crust mess off, I discovered my fingertips were stained black with ink. I really was quite the sight. I carefully brushed off the crumbs, working gingerly so I didn't get ink on my gown, then hurried to Mister Denick's stall.

A sign reading "The Great Library of Alexandria" hung above the door to his stall. Grinning happily, I went inside.

"Ah, Isabelle," Mister Denick said. "Come, come. Have a look," he said, lifting a crate of books and setting it on the counter.

I gasped. "All new? Wherever did you get them?" I asked as I unpacked the two books I had borrowed from Mister Denick last week.

"A gentleman was auctioning off some books from the estate of Horace Walpole, the gentleman who owned Strawberry Hill out in Twickenham."

"The same gentleman who wrote *The Castle of Otranto*?"

"The very same!" Mister Denick said, clapping his hands together excitedly. "I got this lot for a bargain. They went quickly, but there are some gems in here. Have a look."

I picked up each book carefully. Many written in Greek or Latin. There were a few obscure reads, one on Sumerian religions, another on Russian folklore, but then I spotted two that piqued my curiosity. "These," I said, setting aside a book about goblins and another on mythical artifacts. "May I borrow them?"

Mister Denick nodded. "Of course, of course. And I found this for you at an auction on Monday," he said, setting down a book with a blue leather spine. "It's in Latin, but it chronicles the inventions of Hero of Alexandria."

Gasping, I picked up the book and flipped open the page. My eyes rested on the description of a device called an aeolipile. "Oh, isn't this amazing?" I gushed. Hero of Alexandria described a device unlike anything I had ever seen before. I hugged the book to my chest. "Thank you so much."

Master Denick laughed. "Of course, of course."

"I must keep this volume," I said, gazing down at the book once more. "What are you asking for this gem?"

"Nothing, my dear. But, if you have a few moments, my clock isn't keeping the correct time again. And my lamp started flickering."

I set my basket on the counter and pulled out the small toolkit from inside. "Lead the way."

2
LEBOUEF

It took about an hour to complete all the repairs. Finishing the lamp was easy, but repairing Mister Denick's clock proved more difficult. It was the third time I'd worked on it. The antique beauty was simply wearing out. I always carried a few extra bits and bobs in my basket, which did the trick to keep it running for now, but he would soon need me to rework a section of the inner cogs and coils.

"When Papa and I return from our trip, I'll make a complete repair," I said wiping my hands off on a rag.

"As bad as that?" Mister Denick asked, eyeing the clock skeptically.

"Rusted and old, that's all."

"Ah! Just like me."

I chuckled.

"I won't see you again before your trip. I do wish you and your father a fair voyage."

"Thank you, sir. And again, thank you for the books."

The man bowed. "It's my pleasure, Miss Hawking. I do believe you are the most well-read woman in London."

I laughed. "A compliment, I know, but I suspect it makes me a bit odd."

"Odd? Well, who likes ordinary anyway?"

"True. Very true. And again, thank you," I said, patting my basket which was now full of books. I headed back into the market following the aisles toward Tinker's Hall.

I wove through the labyrinth of stalls. The place was crowded, vendors and buyers haggling over the price of everything from eggs to art. Glad to get out of the general crowd, I breathed a sigh of relief when I arrived at Tinker's Hall. There, the most ingenious craftsman, clockwork designers, engineers, fireworks vendors, and airship parts salesmen could be found. Tinker's Hall was unlike anywhere else in London. It was a place where all the great masters gathered. From designing the next best airship to working on steam-powered vehicles to tinkering with automatons, this was the place everyone who had a heart for mechanics loved. Everyone, including me.

I passed the replica of Tinker's Tower at the entrance of the hall then went in search of my father.

"Good morning, Miss Isabelle," Budgie, one of the airship parts vendors, called. Budgie and my father were close friends. Long ago, my father had been one of the most well-noted airship designers in London. But an accident had cost him—and me—the one thing we valued most: my mother. My parents were ingenious airship designers, but with all new inventions, there was the potential for mistakes. A flaw in the design of an airship that my parents had invented resulted in the crash that had killed my mother. Since then, Papa never looked at, boarded, or even talked about airships.

I waved to Budgie, eyeing the airship captain talking to Budgie's assistant. The airship captain was a burly creature with rugged good looks, just the kind of man I'd do best to avoid. Airship captains were usually pirates, half-pirates, scoundrels, or company men. Given the proportions, on the whole, they were more bad than good.

Moving on, I worked my way through the hall. At one stall, a man was working on a backpack rigged with some sort of booster engine. It looked like…someone was going to die or, at least set their trousers on fire. Another man was wearing goggles that amplified his eyes ten-fold as he worked on a tiny clockwork device. I paused and watched another master working on a velocipede attached to a glass globe. The two-wheeled machine was held stationary while a young man pedaled; the tinker adjusted some wires connected to the device. In fits and spurts, a glass globe flickered to life.

"Hello, Miss Hawking," a sultry voice whispered in my ear. A red rose suddenly appeared over my shoulder. "For you."

I exhaled heavily. "Hello, Gerard," I said, stepping away. The smell of cologne nearly overwhelmed me. I tried to plaster on a fake smile, but failed. I turned to find Gerard LeBoeuf standing far too close to me.

He pressed the rose toward me again. "Please, *ma cherie*. For the most beautiful girl in London."

I bit the inside of my cheek and debated. It was far easier to accept the gift rather than put up with the display he'd put on if I didn't. Besides, it was just a rose. What harm could a single rose cause? And while I had no interest in Gerard LeBoeuf, I wouldn't be cruel. He was an enthusiastic suitor. And, given he was also the most gifted cartographer in the realm, he was a man of some quality. Unfortunately, his merits weren't what I was looking for in a man. I wanted someone reserved: quiet, considerate, even a bit shy. I wanted someone the complete opposite of Gerard LeBoeuf. "Thank you, Gerard," I said politely. "That's very kind of you."

He smiled happily, a glimmer of hope in his eyes. He turned to look at the velocipede. "Fascinating, isn't it?" he said, nodding with his chin toward the device. He set his hand on my shoulder and moved close to me once more. "See there," he added, pointing. "The friction from the velocipede moves through the conductor and—"

"Yes, Gerard. I understood. It is very fascinating. Now, if you will excuse me, I should find Papa," I said then turned away, heading back into the hall.

To my horror, he followed me. "So, I understand you and Master Hawking are going on a trip. Scotland, is it? Or was it Ireland? How could you leave without telling me? What will I do without seeing your beautiful face every Wednesday?"

I rolled my eyes. "I'm sure you will find something else to keep you distracted." Namely, the next pretty woman who walked through the hall.

"But Isabelle, there is no better distraction than you. I tell all my friends, 'Wednesday is my favorite day of the week.' And they ask me 'Why?' I tell them 'Because Isabelle Hawking comes to Tinker's Hall. She is the most beautiful girl in London. She has a cute little walk, hair brown as a chestnut, and big curious eyes. She is the perfect woman.' They call me a man in love. Maybe I am. I don't know. But I do know that sometimes Isabelle Hawking comes to Tinker's Hall, and sometimes she even smiles at me," he said, setting his hand on the small of my back. Well, not quite the small of my back—somewhere a bit lower.

Stopping, I frowned at him.

"Alas. Not today."

"Kindly remove your hand," I said, helping him move his paw from my backside. "No, not today. Not next week. Not next year. Now, if you please," I said then turned and walked away.

To my surprise, however, Gerard reached out for my hand. "Miss Hawking, please. I would die for you, don't you see?"

Gasping, surprised by the strength of his grasp and the firmness of grip, I twitched my fingers, activating a lever that caused a spring inside my ring, which was shaped like a hedge-hog, to pop up. Needle-sharp spines pierced Gerard's hand, fending off his unwanted touch.

"Ouch!" Gerard said, pulling his hand back.

I gave him a hard look.

He laughed. "Oh, Miss Hawking, you are so clever," he said as he sucked the blood from the wound between his thumb and forefinger. "You will put up a fight, eh? Not so easily won? Good! I need a woman with a spine of steel and skin like silk. You are perfect in every way, Isabelle Hawking. You must marry me, Isabelle. Say yes."

Gasping, I stared at him. "You must be joking."

Gerard laughed again. "Please, Isabelle. I love you!"

At this point, I realized that several of the shoppers and vendors had stopped to watch the exchange. I exhaled deeply, feeling a flash of angry red burn in my cheeks then turned away from him. An elderly woman who was watching the exchange chuckled then winked at me. Glaring at Gerard, I handed the rose to her then stalked off.

"Isabelle," Gerard called.

I didn't look back.

"Isabelle, marry me. Please?"

I rolled my eyes and kept walking.

"Give up, LeBoeuf," one of the tinkers called with a laugh.

"Not today, LeBeouf," another added.

"Never," a third called.

"Marry me! I'll marry you," the old woman called then cackled loudly.

I glanced over my shoulder.

The old woman was waving the rose toward Gerard.

Gerard turned on his heel and headed back to his own stall.

Sometimes it didn't pay to be nice. Gerard was perfect on the outside, but inside he was a slimy rat. I was growing tired of his romantic jokes and pawing hands. It was one thing if he wanted to court me properly, but such outlandish exchanges were just vulgar. I felt embarrassed.

Shaking my head, I moved toward the back of the hall where my father usually lingered. Of all the men in London, why did Gerard LeBoeuf have to set his cap toward me? I mean, it would be nice to have a suitor, but not *him*. I'd thought I'd found a match with the brooding but kind Doctor Murray. The doctor had frequented my home and was a friend of my father's. He was the perfect man: intelligent, handsome, and reserved. But I should have known Doctor Murray was in love with his childhood friend, Elyse McKenna. My affection for Doctor Murray had been entirely one-sided. My hopes had come to nothing. I couldn't begrudge Doctor Murray and Miss McKenna—well, she was Missus Murray now. I had never seen a happier couple. I only hoped that I could find a love like that one day.

Shaking off the encounter with Gerard, I headed toward the back of Tinker's Hall. There, I spotted my father talking to one of the craftsmen.

"Ah, here you are, my dear. Two centimeters and as slim as can be," my father said, handing a package containing a glass cylinder to me.

"Wherever did you find one?"

"Find? Oh no, my girl. The Wizard of Glass blew the piece just for you," he said, waving to Vinicio Bintello, a Venetian glassblower, four stalls down.

I waved in thanks to the man then turned to my father once more. "Thank you, Papa."

"Of course! Now, do you need anything else? This will be your last chance to shop before we set sail Friday."

I shook my head. For months, Papa and I had been working on a series of commissions for a Scottish nobleman. He had met my father and me in London in the autumn and had fallen in love with our work. Certain his new wife, who was a connoisseur of fine art, would love my clockwork sculptures, he'd commissioned clocks from my father and art pieces from me. The work had taken months, but we were finally ready. Now that I had the glass cylinder, I had everything I needed. The wedding was just a week away. Papa and I would sail to the Isle of Islay on Friday to deliver our creations. I was beyond excited. Not only were we planning to attend the wedding, but Papa had also arranged for us to participate in a symposium in Belfast where we would meet with renowned Irish tinkers.

It was the trip of a lifetime.

I could hardly wait.

3
LOVE'S BLOOM

AFTER WE FINISHED UP AT THE MARKET, PAPA AND I WALKED home to our workshop between London and Blackfriar's bridges along the Thames. As we walked, I flipped through the pages of the book on the ancient inventor Hero of Alexandria. The book chronicled the man's inventions, though the details of how the machines worked lacked specificity.

"Apple?" Papa offered as we walked, pulling a green apple from his pocket.

I nodded, slipping my basket to the crook of my arm so I could eat and walk at the same time.

Papa took a bite of his own apple as he rolled a round device in his hand.

"What are you reading, dearest?" he asked.

"Mmm? Oh, a treatise on Hero of Alexandria."

"Hero of Alexandria. I believe I saw a reference to him in one of McGill's essays. McGill, always spouting off about this or that ancient inventor. He'll be at the symposium, you know. Shall I have a look at the text when you're done? Perhaps I can find something McGill hasn't read before."

I chuckled at Papa's propensity for professional rivalry. "Of course. And just what are you rolling around?"

"Master Bintello blew me a glass orb," he said, lifting the glass and holding it toward the sky. He squinted one eye as he looked through the sphere.

"You have a hundred such orbs."

"Not like this, my dear. Look," he said, handing it to me.

I lifted the orb and looked through it. I was surprised to see that the reflection in the distance was reversed. I gasped. "Now, how did he manage that?"

Papa chuckled. "A glassblower's secret."

I handed the orb back to Papa. "Ingenious."

"Now, let me see what I can make of it."

While my father's formal trade had shifted from airships to clocks, his genius led him in new, exciting directions. He'd been working on creating devices that could help the sick and maimed. He'd become practically obsessed with building an optic that could work to replace a human eye. His interest in all things medical was how I'd come to meet Doctor Murray. The doctor's knowledge of the human body coupled with my father's sense of the mechanical made them a good match. Good for my father. Alas, not a match for me.

My thoughts went to LeBoeuf once more. I shuddered. How could a man be so perfect on the outside and so sloppy on the inside? I guess what they said was true, beauty was only skin deep.

I turned back to my book and took another bite of the apple.

Following the twists and turns of the London streets, soon we arrived home. I smiled up at the face of our little workshop facing the Thames. I was going to miss the view and comforts of home. But still, an adventure at sea and a lordly wedding were enough to get me to leave home without too much complaining.

Papa and I let ourselves in. Papa held his apple in his mouth while he pulled off his coat. The sight made me giggle.

"You look like a pig ready for the spit. Here," I said, setting down my book and basket so I could help him shrug off his jacket.

Once he was free of his wraps, Papa removed the apple. "Thank you, dearest. Now, anything else you need from outside? A bonnet? Perhaps some ink? What about your dress for the wedding?"

"Delivered yesterday."

"And did you go with the pink or the green?"

"Yellow."

"Yellow. Very good. Anything else then?"

I shook my head. "My trunks are already packed. One for clothes. One for tools and books."

"Very good. Very good. The workers will be by to collect the clocks and sculptures. Do you have everything ready?"

I nodded. "One last check and a minor adjustment now that I have this," I said, lifting the glass cylinder.

With that, my father nodded. "Very well. I won't keep you then." Leaning in, he kissed me on the cheek then headed toward his workshop in the basement. I grabbed my books and basket and went to my workshop at the back of the house. There, I had a good view of the garden. The sunny space was perfect. The ample sunlight allowed me to see the inner workings of my designs more easily. And since most of my work was inspired by nature, I loved being under the sky. The workshop was—so my father told me time and time again—my mother's favorite space in the whole house. Though she died when I was very little, being there made me feel close to her, like she was watching me, helping me with my creations.

I met Martin, our footman, in the hall. "Miss Hawking, welcome home. Shall I arrange for some tea?"

"Please! And some sandwiches? Do we have any salted pork left? And cheese?"

"Yes, miss. I'll see to it."

"And a tray for my father as well, please. In our workshops."

"Of course."

I headed toward the back. Sunlight streamed in through the windows. I stepped around the tall palm plant and went to the table where all my commissioned designs sat ready. Three sculptures were completed. The fourth sat waiting on my workbench. I eyed over the designs.

The first was a sculpture that appeared to be silver birds roosting on a tree branch, but when the windup key was turned, the birds sprang to life and sang Vivaldi's *Allegro-Largo-Allegro*.

The second piece was a diorama of ice skaters spinning around a frozen lake. Using mirrors, I'd worked the device to shine sunlight onto the metal trees, making the crystalline snow I'd crafted shimmer with sparkling light. Like the bird sculpture, this piece also played music. This time, the tune was *The First Noel*.

Another of my designs was, in truth, my all-time favorite. It depicted a man and woman seated at a dining table. The couple, both made of bronze, were frozen in the expressions of laughing merriment. I turned the windup key then stood back. Suddenly, the table came to life. A feisty alehouse song played as the dishes on the table began to move in their groves, dancing across the table in interweaving patterns. The candelabra at the center of the table and the teapot danced around one another like they were at a country ball. The couple seated at the table swung their tankards as they watched the show. I chuckled. Dancing dishes. I hoped the lord and lady would like the quaint mirth I'd tried to capture in the piece. The music died down, and the bronze couple returned to their frozen positions, the cutlery and fine china behaving once more. I smiled at the design. Part music box, part clockwork display, it was fully of whimsy.

Turning, I went to my workbench where my last piece sat waiting.

At first blush, it seemed like a simple sculpture. A couple sat on a swing below an arbor of roses. The clockwork pieces had all been working perfectly, but my marriage of music to the movements had lacked an enchanting cadence.

Sliding my stool up to my bench, I opened the metal compartment underneath the sculpture. Pulling on a pair of goggles and dropping down the lenses to the most enlarging lens, I pulled out my tools and got to work replacing the brass cylinder I had been using with the glass piece Papa had commissioned at the market. It was delicate work, but with a little concentration, I'd have it in no time.

At some point, Martin must have come in with the tray. The wafting scent of freshly brewed Earl Grey tea distracted me for a moment, but I just about had the cylinder in place. I pushed my hunger pangs aside and focused on my work. I removed the tiny pins and screws, replaced the piece, then set in the new equipment. Testing the music pins, and adjusting for tone, I finally had it.

With a heavy exhale, I leaned back. I pushed my goggles onto my head and set down my tools. Reaching behind me, I grabbed the cup of tea only to find it was ice cold.

I flicked an eye toward the sky overhead. Was it already late afternoon?

I eyed the plate on the tray. I somewhat remembered seeing a bun there. The plate of food sitting behind me now, however, consisted of fruit, cheese, and nuts. Had Martin cleared the other plate or had I eaten? I couldn't remember.

I grabbed a piece of cheese then reached forward and wound the machine.

The sound of Bach's flute sonata, this time in E minor, filled the workshop.

I smiled.

One part, at least, was done.

Setting the tea back on the tray, I popped the cheese into my mouth then set to work once more. I reattached the music device to the rest of the clockwork gears inside the sculpture. It took some time, but finally, I managed to get everything aligned. Once it was done, I was ready to try it out once more.

"Isabelle?" Papa called. "Are you here?"

"Yes, Papa."

My father joined me at my workbench. "I'm told we missed lunch, but dinner will be served in ten minutes if you'd like to get ready. Well, how is it? Still B flat or did we achieve E minor?"

I turned the key then stood back.

Once again, Bach's sonata started, but this time the entire sculpture came to life. The handsome gentleman stood, his hands behind his back, in a formal posture—a pose I'd modeled after Doctor Murray—and his lover on the swing began swinging back and forth. I'd used a very light weave of silver and silk string for the woman's dress to give it movement. As it was, the music box was sweet, but a moment later, the magic happened. As the song shifted, the design reacted. The tiny metal rosebuds on the arbor slowly opened into large blossoms as if they were blooming in time with the music.

"Love's bloom," I said, watching my creation work.

As the tune slowed, the swing came to a stop, and the metal gentleman leaned down to kiss his lover. I watched the pair carefully. It had taken hours to time that movement just right. For at least a month my gentleman had banged his lady on the head, got stuck on the swing, kissed the air behind her, or just plain missed with the same lack of decorum as LeBoeuf. But today, his kiss landed true. The couple kissed. The roses closed once more. The gentleman and lady return to their waiting postures.

My father wrapped his arm around my waist. "This is... It's just wonderful."

I pulled out the windup key. "So much magic in one turn of the key."

My father shook his head. "The magic is here," he said, taking my hands into his and kissing the backs of my hands.

I giggled.

"Now, let's eat something. Two sleeps, my dear, and the sea will be calling!"

I set the key down on the workbench and looked at my metal lovers. I smiled at them, proud of myself that I was able to render the sweetest of expressions in their gaze. Frozen in silver, they still looked at one another with the expression of complete and total love.

I wished I could find a man who looked at me like that.

4
THE PROSPERO

AFTER DINNER, I WENT BACK TO THE WORKSHOP TO MAKE some final adjustments to my sculptures. I almost hated to give them up, but I took comfort in the thought that they would bring joy to the newlyweds. It was close to midnight when I finally headed upstairs to bed. I flopped onto my bed and pulled out the book on Hero of Alexandria and his aeolipile. I must have dozed off, because I woke the next morning to the sound of men in the house.

"Miss Hawking," Agatha, our maid, called from the other side of my door. "Your father asked me to see if you could come down. They are almost done packing up the clocks. They want to start on your sculptures."

"Coming," I called with a yawn then sat up. No time to change. I smoothed my hair as best I could, pausing just a moment to wash my face and clean my teeth, then headed back downstairs to the workshop. I guess it was a good thing I'd collapsed into bed fully dressed. I'd just reached my studio when the men arrived with the empty packing crates, Papa leading them.

"Ah, Isabelle. Is everything ready?" he asked.

I nodded. "As long as they are packed in ample straw. I took the liberty of wrapping the more delicate pieces in cloth last night."

"Very well," Papa said then turned to the men, indicating that they could begin packing.

I snatched the leather strap on which I'd strung the windup keys from the table. "Thought these were best kept with me. If they get lost, it will take me a week to fashion replacements."

Papa nodded to me. "Very good. Now, I will accompany these gentlemen to the shipyard to see the pieces and our trunks loaded. Can I bring you anything back?"

"No, Papa," I said, watching anxiously as the men lifted the sculpture with the little birds, setting it gently down in the straw. I held my breath the entire time. I would need to ensure I packed all my tools with me. If the boxes were rattled too hard, I might need to make a quick repair when we arrived.

"Anything for the trip? Sweets, perhaps? A new parasol?"

I laughed. "A parasol? Father, you jest."

"Not at all. It is a wedding, after all, Isabelle. Perhaps you will find someone who catches your eye."

I felt a blush rise up on my cheeks when one of the workers gave me a passing glance.

"And what shall I do, bash him on the head with the handle of my parasol and drag him off?"

At that, both of the men packing up my sculptures chuckled.

Papa joined in the laughter. "Quite right. I don't know. I thought maybe you could twirl it or some such," he said, giving off the air of a refined lady twirling her parasol while bending her neck in the most attractive of poses.

At that, the workers and I chuckled. "No, Papa. I have all I need right here."

"Hmm," Papa mused. "Perhaps LeBoeuf has won your heart after all."

"Papa! Really."

My father pinched my cheek. "My good girl. As you wish, no parasols."

I smiled at him but was grateful when the conversation turned away from my prospects—or the lack thereof save LeBoeuf—to the wooden crates and the size of the storage hold on the ship.

I stayed in the workshop until the last sculpture was taken to the waiting wagon outside. I followed Papa and the workers out front. The boxed pieces and our trunks sat ready.

"Very good," Papa said then crawled into the back of the wagon. "I'll see these secured then be back. See you this afternoon," he said, waving to me.

I gave him a wave then headed back inside.

Papa was right. A wedding was an excellent opportunity to meet someone. But then what? I wanted to be loved. Everyone did. But at what cost? I loved my little home along the Thames. I loved my daily work. I loved going to the market on Wednesday—save the encounters with LeBoeuf—and I enjoyed chatting with Papa about our work. I needed someone who understood the life of a tinker, not someone who expected me to twirl a parasol and crane my neck until my bones cracked. Perhaps the wedding would yield no results, but the symposium in Belfast might. A gathering of the most celebrated minds in all of Ireland was anticipated. The Celtic Clockworks, as they called the learned society in Ireland, was home to many bright minds. Maybe amongst them I would find someone.

And if I did, then what? I looked down at my dress. I was still wearing the same gown I had worn yesterday, and I was covered in gear grease. I should at least prepare myself with a proper bath. Parasol or no, it wouldn't hurt to dig the grime out from under my fingernails and sweeten my hair with a little perfume in preparation for the trip. How were fashionable ladies wearing their hair these days? I wasn't sure.

As I headed upstairs to tidy myself up, I thought about Doctor Murray's wife, Elyse. She was a well-noted actress and always seemed to be fashionably dressed. Did she wear her hair up or pinned at the nape? Some days, I truly missed the mother I never knew.

AFTER LINGERING IN A LONG BATH, during which I read three chapters of the little tome on goblins from Horace Walpole's collection—an interesting fiction piece that read like a spell-book—I went to my chamber and styled my hair, trimmed my nails, and dressed for the day. Of course, it was already after lunch, but no matter. I then went to the workshop, where I cleaned up my bench, packing the tools I would carry with me. I left my toolbox in the foyer then went into the kitchen, where I stole a hunk of bread and some cheese then headed back to my room. Slipping into a window seat that looked out over the Thames, I opened up the goblin book once more.

It was dusk when Papa returned. I spotted him walking down the lane. Setting down my book, I rushed down the steps to meet him at the door.

"Settled. All settled," he said, handing me his hat.

"You smell like the wind," I told him.

He laughed. "What an odd thing to say."

"Well, I am an odd girl."

"Who says?"

"Everyone?"

Papa laughed. "What is the use of being ordinary? Come, let's see what there is for supper. *I* smell chicken and potatoes."

Following Papa, I headed into the dining room where the table—well, half the table, as the other half was stacked with books and boxes—was already set.

"Shall we serve dinner now?" Martin asked.

"Indeed, good man. Let's have one last supper before we turn pirate."

I chuckled and slipped into the seat beside Papa. "Now, tell me, how is the ship?"

"A ship, all in all. Stout and seaworthy. But you do know how I hate sailing."

"Sailing. And flying. And riding. And motoring."

"We have feet. Why not use those?"

"Papa," I said with a laugh, reaching out to squeeze his hand. I knew better than to press the subject. I knew very well why he would not fly.

"Now, in the morning, Doctor Murray and his wife will come to see us off. I need to pass Doctor Murray some papers. He'll be taking care of some business for me in our absence. And then we will sail on the morning tide."

I felt a knot form in my stomach. The sense of disappointment still lingered. I needed to let it go. "Very well. And our ship? On which vessel are we sailing?"

"The *Prospero.*"

"The *Prospero,*" I repeated.

"May she help us prosper!"

"Indeed."

"Here you are, sir," Martin said as he entered the dining room pushing a serving cart.

"Very good, very good," Papa said, slipping his napkin into the collar of his shirt.

Martin set out our plates, poured us some wine, then departed.

"To the *Prospero,*" Papa said, lifting his glass.

"To the *Prospero,*" I repeated, toasting him. "May good fortune be ours."

Papa and I *clinked* our glasses then drank.

Tomorrow was going to be an exciting day.

5
THE MIRROR

THERE WAS A FLURRY OF ACTIVITY AROUND THE *PROSPERO* AS the ship prepared for departure. I stood at the side of the ship looking out at the Thames. The wind tugged on my blue traveling coat and made the skirts of my yellow dress flutter all around me. I held on to the rail of the ship. Tremors of excitement ran through my body.

"Isabelle," Papa called, crossing the deck toward me. "Doctor and Missus Murray are here. They wanted to wish you farewell," he said, motioning back to the handsome couple standing beside a carriage not far from the dock.

My heart skipped a beat when I saw Doctor Murray. What a fine figure he cut in his top hat and dark coat. Elyse, his wife, waved to me. I sighed.

"Very well," I said then rushed down the plank to meet them.

They smiled at me.

"We are nearly ready. I've never been at sea before. Papa tells me I will adore it. But I will miss you both," I said happily as I approached. My stomach knotted, the ache of jealousy trying to form once more.

"I have a small gift for you. For luck," Elyse—Missus Murray—said, handing me an item wrapped in a pretty silk scarf. The scarf itself was gift enough. I smiled at her. She was kind, and beautiful, and talented. She was so...*perfect*. It would be easy to hate her. But how could I? She had never meant to do me any harm. I cast a glance at Doctor Murray who favored me with a small smile—that was all I could ever get out of him. I suppressed a defeated sigh.

I opened the package. Inside, was a small hand mirror. "This workmanship," I said, tracing my finger along the silver filigree. "I've never seen anything like it!" And I honestly had not. Not even the finest jewel crafters in London could make such a detailed, exquisite piece.

"It's quite magical. I'm told that if you look into this mirror under the light of the moon, it will show you your heart's desire," Elyse said.

Was she joking? I looked up at her, studying her face. An actress by trade, she could hold any expression she chose with conviction. But she seemed quite serious.

"You jest, I know, but what a fascinating idea. Elyse, I cannot accept this. It's too—"

"I don't need it anymore. I have my heart's desire," she said, beaming up at Doctor Murray.

Was she trying to hurt my feelings? I knew she suspected my unreturned affection for Doctor Murray, but I'd never known her to be cruel. I studied her face once more. Again, I saw that same honest expression. No, she wasn't trying to hurt me. She was just...in love. I looked back at the mirror.

"Safe travels, Miss Hawking," Doctor Murray said.

"Isabelle! We're ready," Papa called from the ship. He beckoned to me.

"Time to go," I whispered, clutching the mirror my chest. I looked at Elyse once more. She smiled at me in all sincerity. The mirror really was lovely, and it was a thoughtful gift. "I promise to keep your magic mirror with me at all times," I said with a light laugh.

Elyse smiled.

"Doctor Murray," I said, dropping a curtsey. "*Missus* Murray." I smiled at them both, gave a little wave, then turned and ran back to the ship, joining Papa once more.

We both waved to the couple then turned to settle in for the trip.

"What's this?" he asked, looking down at the bundle in my hands.

I handed the mirror to him. "My goodness," he said, looking at the silverwork.

"A gift from Missus Murray."

"It's remarkable. I wonder where she got it."

I chuckled. "She said it's magic."

"Actresses…professional liars," he said with a good-natured laugh. "She is a sweet lady. And very thoughtful."

"Sir. We are ready to depart," one of the sailors said. "Perhaps you and your daughter would be more comfortable below deck with the other passengers?"

"Good God, man. No. We'll stay here—out of the way, I assure you—and have a look."

The sailor gave me a passing glance but simply nodded to my father and went on his way.

"Come," Papa said, leading me to a spot along the rail away from the flurry of activity. We settled in on a box and watched as they unmoored the vessel.

The wind whipped harshly, pulling my dark locks from my long braid.

I set the mirror in my lap and used the pretty scarf, which was trimmed in purple and blue roses, to cover my hair.

Papa looked at me then chuckled. "We should have bought you a proper traveling bonnet."

"What? You don't like my babushka? Agatha would be proud."

Papa laughed again then pinched my cheek. "How like your mother you are at times. Always full of mirth."

I smiled then took his hand and gave it a squeeze. I stared out at the Thames, wondering for the thousandth time about my mother, a mysterious but omnipresent figure in my life who, at least for me, had never really existed. I gazed down at the mirror in my lap, wishing Elyse's magic mirror could show my mother to me.

Catching the bright light of the sun, the mirror glimmered brightly, shining in my eyes. In that odd moment, I could have sworn I'd seen something in the looking glass, but the light passed, and only the blinding sun was there. Magic indeed. I turned the mirror over, covering the light, and stared out at the Thames, knowing there was no way for my wish to ever come true.

6
THE TEMPEST

THE CAPTAIN INFORMED US THAT THE TRIP WOULD TAKE THE entire day and evening. "The moon will be out when we pull into port tomorrow night. But barring any bad weather, we should arrive on schedule," the man informed my father as he passed by.

The sights and sounds of the ship were fascinating. I spent the morning on the deck watching the sailors work, enjoying the view as the Thames slipped past and we put out to sea. It had occurred to me on several occasions that if we'd taken a coach to Wales, or even gone by motor, we would have saved ourselves a considerable amount of time, but I said nothing to Papa. He had his reasons, and I understood him well.

There were ten other passengers onboard, most of whom stayed below deck even as the ship rounded Cornwall, moving from the Channel north. It was a shame. They were missing everything. I slid my hand over the rail and felt the spray of the dark blue water on my palm.

"Look, Papa," I said happily, spying a pod of dolphins. Their fins wove in and out of the water between the waves as they swam alongside the ship. One of the creatures leaped from the depths below, jumping over and over again as it played with the waves. It came so close to the side of the boat that I could see its dark eye glancing at me.

"Curious creature," Papa said. "Just look at him."

Laughing, I waved to the dolphin. Eventually, the pod swam off, leaving me with an idea.

"Oh, Papa, what a wonderful sculpture it would make, dolphins swimming amongst pitching waves," I said, quickly pulling out my notebook and turning to a blank page.

"I can see it now, my dear," Papa said as he lit his pipe and settled in with his book once more.

I spent the rest of the afternoon and into the early evening drawing my new design. It was only when the light grew dim after sunset that I realized it was time to go below deck.

"Well, my dear, I can't read another word in this light," Papa said.

"I was beginning to come to the same conclusion," I said, closing my journal.

"The waves have begun to toss a bit. Shall we go below?"

I nodded.

At that, we found our way to the quarters. Papa was right. The waves had grown rough as night had fallen. Bracing myself so I didn't tumble, I descended the narrow steps below deck. In the mess hall, the others were settling in for a meager dinner. Papa and I went first to our small cabin.

"Dinner, Isabelle?" Papa asked as he washed his hands with the small pitcher of water on a narrow basin.

I shook my head. "I think I'll rest instead."

"Very well. Let me see what kind of wine they have. All this heaving is giving me a bit of a headache."

At that, he left me.

I crawled up onto my bunk. The mattress was overly stiff, but the sea air had made me tired. I stuffed my journal into my bag with my books and Elyse's mirror then closed my eyes. I must have fallen asleep quickly, and deeply, because I didn't fully wake again. Sometime that evening, I heard Papa return. He was talking about the weather taking a turn, but said not to worry. Seeing that I was still mostly asleep, he didn't push the conversation further. I heard him crawl into his bunk below, mumbling about how hard the bed was. I didn't hear anything else. Instead, I was lost in dreams.

IT WAS the strangeness of the sound that first woke me. I was dreaming I was in a forest. Somewhere, far in the distance, a tree fell, and a woman screamed. That seemed odd to me. Then I heard a scream again followed by the sound of rough voices shouting orders.

"What in the devil?" Papa said as he woke.

The ship pitched sideways, and in my sleepy state, I rolled out of the cot and hit the floor. My eyes only opened just in time to see my bag come sliding toward me.

Gasping, I leaped forward to catch it before Elyse's mirror shattered into a thousand pieces.

The ship pitched once again, and I fell backward.

"Isabelle," Papa called, reaching out to me.

"I'm all right," I called as I braced myself against the wall.

"Hard port! Hard port!" I heard someone scream overhead.

Then there was a terrible jolt as the ship slammed into something.

A moment later, water began leaking into the cabin.

"Good God," Papa yelped. Jumping out of bed, he grabbed my hand.

Securing my satchel around me, I followed Papa as he flung open the door. From the other end of the ship in the direction of the mess hall, water filled the boat rapidly.

I gasped. "We're shipwrecked."

We headed quickly up the steps to the deck of the ship. There, I saw the mast had splintered and fallen over the side. And then I saw why.

All around, a wild tempest tossed waves onto the deck of the ship. The battered vessel cracked. The wind whipped horribly, and to my shock, I saw it was heavy with a squall of snow. Holding on to a pole for dear life, I gazed around me in the darkness. The deck of the ship was lit only by two small lanterns. The sailors were working busily trying to get the small life raft ready and load up the first of the passengers.

"Master Hawking! Miss Hawking! Come on," the captain called, waving us to the small boat. The wind whipped ferociously, the snowflakes blinding me. Waves crashed all around, drenching us with cold water as the icy blast froze us.

"Isabelle, come on," Papa said, gripping my hand tightly. Moving carefully, we made our way toward the rowboat.

The sailors tried to hold the small boat steady as the rest of the passengers got on, but a huge wave toppled over the side of the ship, knocking two of the men from their feet, washing them out into the sea. They lost the lead on the boat, and the vessel, carried by the wave, disappeared into the darkness. From where I stood, braced against a pole, I couldn't see if the tiny boat had capsized or not.

Behind me, I heard another terrible crack.

I looked back to see the ship splintering in half.

"This way," Papa called, pulling me toward the front of the ship where the captain and the sailors were readying another rowboat.

Papa and I moved toward them. We were just about there when the ship below us heaved. The wind whipped wildly and a squall of snow blinded me.

And then, a giant wave smashed over the side of the vessel.

I heard the captain scream.

I felt my feet lift off the deck as the wave slammed me into the sea.

I felt Papa's fingers leave my grasp as the sea violently tore our hands apart.

Something hit me hard on the back of the head.

Then there was nothing.

7
SHIPWRECKED

"SHE HAS WINDUP KEYS."

"I see. I see. Look! Look! She's wearing keys."

"She's waking up."

"Go. Go."

I coughed hard and spit up water. My lungs ached. I slowly opened my eyes. I was lying on a rocky beach. Water lapped at my feet. I coughed again, clearing out the last of the briny water from my mouth, nose, and lungs. I sat up slowly, the world around me slowly coming into focus. The back of my head hurt, and the strain of my eyes told me I had hit my head hard.

Sitting up, I looked around me.

Debris from the shipwreck littered the beach. Gazing out at the waves, I saw nothing on the horizon. The pebbly beach was entirely deserted save the wreckage and me. I looked behind me to see a dense forest. The shoreline was shrouded in fog, but it was not snowing. In fact, it felt like a warm spring morning, the air damp with dense fog.

I was surprised to find my satchel was still strung around me.

Legs shaking, I rose. My head swam dizzily, and for a moment, I thought I might be ill. Scanning around, I spotted a tall stick. I picked it up then braced myself against it as I took in my surroundings.

There was nothing here save the wind, the sea, and the forest.

I gazed out at the waves once more. While there was no sign of the ship, I did spot the dorsal fins of dolphins swimming not far from shore.

Steadying myself, I turned back toward the shoreline.

Papa. I needed to find Papa.

"Hello?" I called.

My voice echoed across a vast empty space.

In the forest, a flock of birds was startled by the sound of my voice. They flew off. Otherwise, it was eerily silent. Yet I couldn't shake the sense that someone was close by.

"Hello? Anyone?" I called again.

No one answered.

I glanced at the beach. All manner of clothes, ropes, splinters of wood, and even a tobacco tin had floated to the shore. There could be others like me who'd washed up on the beach. I needed to look. Someone may be hurt...or worse. Papa. I needed to find Papa or the next village down the shore or something.

Leaning against the tall staff, I began walking down the pebbly beach. The rocks on the shoreline were round and black and worn smooth by the relentless waves. My head ached, and my legs felt weak, but I kept moving.

"Papa? Papa?" I called, looking toward the dense forest. The woods were thick with massive oak trees. I couldn't remember ever seeing such wide trunks before. It would take three men to reach their arms around them. The fog shifted on the ground below the trees. It was so dark in the forest, but then I heard *something*, like the tinkling of a small silver bell.

"Hello?" I called.

For the life of me, I could have sworn I heard a child's laughter.

"Hello? Is there anyone there?"

But there was nothing save a warm wind that made the broad green leaves on the trees wave and the tall grass bend in the breeze. But when it did so, the grass revealed a stone poking out of the ground. I could see it was carved.

Maybe a road marker?

I stepped into the grass at the edge of the forest then pushed the blades, nearly jumping out of my skin when I found a face looking back at me. The stone was, in fact, an old Celtic marker. Someone had carved a face into the stone. Slash marks lined the side of the rock. There were Ogham marks, the language of the ancient Celts. I recognized it but couldn't read it.

"Where am I, ancient friend?" I whispered to the stone then rose, leaning heavily against my staff. My head swam, black dots appearing before my eyes. I took a moment to steady myself then went back to the beach. Moving slowly, I walked along the shoreline. Signs of the shipwreck were abundant, but there was no sign of anyone else.

"Hello? Anyone?"

Feeling weak and cold, I made my way along until the land narrowed to a long point. Soon, I found myself standing on a bar of pebbles. I cast my eyes out at the water. There was nothing. Nothing. Was I facing England and Scotland or was I facing Ireland?

I turned and looked back. From this vantage point, I expected to see the shoreline trimming the horizon on either side. But instead, I found water on *both* sides of the narrow point. Good lord, I was on an island. Had we passed the Isle of Man or was I elsewhere? There were so many small islands in the narrow sea between England and Ireland. I could be…anywhere.

"Hello?"

Once more, the wind rustled the leaves, but there was no answer.

Following the shoreline again, I made my way up the beach. Here, the signs of the shipwreck were far fewer. I eyed the coastline for any sign of a house or wharf, but there was nothing but the dense forest and the waves. I felt dizzy. Whatever I'd hit or had hit me had done so with terrible force. Stopping, I bent over to catch my breath. My stomach rolled once more, and I thought I might be sick.

The wind blew again, and this time, I could have sworn I heard voices.

Leaning heavily against my makeshift staff, I stared into the woods. "Who's there?" I called.

The hairs on the back of my neck rose, and my skin turned to gooseflesh.

This time, when the wind rustled the leaves, I spied a worn path hidden by the long blades of grass. Once upon a time, the earth had been trampled down here by foot or hoof. The trail led into the forest. I stared into the dark woods. My mind split with two ideas. Something called to me, urging me to venture into the woods. Yet another instinct told me to stay away. In the end, I headed back up the beach away from the path. I eyed the woods warily. Maybe the path would have led to an old woodcutter's house or perhaps a fisherman's hut. But something felt off.

As I walked up the beach, I remembered reading the stories of the Roman invasion of Celtic Britain. Hadn't the Celtic tribes had sacred islands offshore from which they'd called upon their gods to save them from the Romans? I remembered the story of the Romans shaking in fear as the Druids of old—priests and priestesses—called upon their magic to save them from the invaders. My skin prickled at the thought. I was making myself nervous.

I headed back up the beach. The debris from the shipwreck was on one side of the island only, but in my confused state, I wasn't sure if it was east or west. The dense fog occluded the sun. My temples throbbing, I doubted my natural sense of north and south—and my true sense of direction had always been good. As more time passed, my headache began to blind me, and my stomach ached. Did I have a concussion?

Black spots appeared before my eyes, and my stomach pitched again.

This time, I did get sick. Leaning into the bushes, I vomited up the last of the seawater and stomach acid. I clung to the walking stick as I swayed.

I needed to go back to the main site of the wreckage. My best chance was to try to make a fire and stay there. And I needed to rest.

Gathering myself, I headed out once more.

The day passed, and it began to grow dim. I neither heard nor saw any other living person…save the odd sounds in the woods. No doubt those were just hallucinations in my concussed state.

Out of desperation and frustration, tears pricked the corners of my eyes.

"Papa?" I called, my voice dry and raspy. "Papa?"

Terror swept over me.

With each step, I failed to find my father. What if… What if he'd been lost at sea?

That was a thought I could not bear. I could not live without my father. He was all I had. Tears streamed down my cheeks.

Once again, I spotted the debris from the ship. But there was no one. There was only me.

A soft moan escaped my lips.

"Papa?" I whispered.

Again, the wind blew.

Once more, the wind revealed another path through the woods. This time, however, I saw that some stones lined the walkway. I eyed the path. Yes, there was very definitely a man-made path here. So, where did it lead?

I stared into the ever-darkening woods.

The massive oak trees swayed in the breeze. In the far distance, I heard a soft chime.

I could follow the path just a little. Maybe there was an old house with a hearth, somewhere to get dry and light a fire, somewhere off the beach. I wouldn't go far, just down the path for a look.

Gathering up my skirts, my petticoat and undergarment still damp, I followed the path into the woods.

It was foggy here, the air shrouded in mist that seemed to weave around the oaks. Taking a deep breath, I headed into the forest. My heart slammed in my chest.

When I stepped between two arching oaks, I felt like I'd been swallowed by the wilderness.

8
THE ISLAND

IT TOOK A MOMENT FOR MY EYES TO ADJUST TO THE DIM
light. The canopy of trees overhead hid what sun there was. I
made out a path in the woods that seemed to
lead…somewhere.

Following the trail, I moved under the tall oaks. The
massive timbers swayed in the breeze. Again, I heard a soft
tinkling sound. The forest, from what I could tell, was
untouched. Maybe I was right to think of the ancient
Romans and Celts. Sunlight slanted through the branches,
casting blobs of golden light on the forest floor. The smell of
the forest—new spring leaves and heady loam—made a sweet
perfume far different from the air in London. It put my unset-
tled head at ease. Motes of dust floated through the air,
making it shimmer. Spring flowers grew in small bunches at
the base of the trees. Mushrooms seemed to grow
everywhere.

I stepped off the path just a moment to look at an impressive ring of red-capped mushrooms growing in a circle. But
then I remembered my fairy tales and Mister Walpole's book
on goblins. It was best not to get too close to a ring of mush-

rooms where faeries danced. I thought again about the book then dug into my satchel.

I was relieved and surprised to find that Elyse's mirror had survived the wreck unscathed. Mister Walpole's books, my journal, and the tome on Hero of Alexandria had not fared as well. All of them were wet. When I was finally settled, I'd need to investigate the damage. But at the moment, I was searching for something else.

At the bottom of my bag, safely stowed, I found the small hairpin I always carried. It was trimmed with a metal bumblebee.

"Pardon," I said, stepping into the ring of mushrooms. Leaning against my staff, I set the hairpin down at the center of the ring. "Faerie troupe, accept my gift, if you please. And if you will, help me find a way to safety and recover Papa."

Moving carefully, I stepped back.

Perhaps it was a superstitious thing to do, but I was lost, and Mister Walpole's book on goblins had undoubtedly enriched my imagination. And this island, well, it just seemed so…

My thoughts left me then as the sun glimmered brightly through the trees far deeper into the forest and I saw a ring of stones.

Gasping, I walked deeper into the forest toward the ring.

Papa and I had talked many times about taking a trip to Salisbury to see the standing stones at Stonehenge. We'd hoped to go this year at midsummer when they said the sky and stones aligned. I had never seen any of the ancient rings before. But there, just before me, in the midst of this forgotten wilderness, was a ring of nine stones.

I approached the stones carefully. I felt their energy, or maybe it was an echo of those who had come before, but once more, my skin prickled to gooseflesh. And, reminding me I was not well, my head swam.

The dark stones were a good three feet taller than I was. Moss and lichen grew on the stones. As I studied them, I saw that they were all carved with Celtic knots and designs, trimmed with Ogham writing, and had faces carved thereon. They were exquisite. I had never even heard of such fabulously decorated stones before.

Taking a deep breath and chiding myself for being overly superstitious—again, I blamed Mister Walpole's book on goblins—I stepped inside the ring of stones.

At the center of the ring, the sunlight shimmered with renewed vigor. There was a feeling of magic in the air. I could hardly breathe. I went from stone to stone studying the faces and designs. A wealth of knowledge, lost lore, was just at my fingertips.

Reaching out carefully, I gently touched the face on one of the monoliths.

The wind blew once more, and this time, I swore I heard voices on the wind.

"Hello? Is anyone there?"

The sky overhead darkened, and in the distance, I heard the rumble of thunder.

Oh no. No, no, no.

I looked up at the sky. My head swam.

I needed to find shelter.

I turned to go back to the path, but when I did so, I didn't see the path, nor the ring of mushrooms, nor anything else vaguely familiar.

Once more, the sky rumbled.

I felt the first of the raindrops on my head, but luckily, the thick leaves overhead sheltered me somewhat. As the storm rolled in, the forest grew dark.

I cast a glance around.

It didn't matter which direction I went. Eventually I would find the shore once more.

Turning to head out, however, I spotted a bluish colored light in the distance. A house? A fire? A lantern? A...*something*.

"Hello?"

No reply.

Turning, I followed the bluish glow. I headed deeper into the forest, chasing after the light, but soon found its source. It was a mushroom. The glowing mushroom had been sitting on a rise. It had played a trick on my mind. Then I spotted another glowing fungus, then another, and another, all of which held an incandescent blue light. They grew in a straight line. Without a better recourse, and feeling half suspicious of the supernatural, I followed the glow of the blue mushrooms as the rain pattered overhead, the sky rumbling. I followed the blue lights deep into the ancient woods, aware that I was passing other sacred rings. I walked past a mound of earth, a barrow, the final resting place of some ancient person—and some said a passageway to the Otherworld—as I hurried deeper into the woods. Surely I would find the shoreline soon.

Lightning cracked overhead.

Then, on the horizon, I saw golden light. A fire? I squinted my eyes, trying to make out the shape through the trees, but my head ached miserably. Leaning heavily against my staff, I moved toward the golden colored light.

The forest thinned. The glowing mushrooms led me onward toward the glow of the yellow light in the distance. Praying to find someone—anyone—I followed along, well aware that my quick exertion had my stomach rolling. Black spots wriggled before my eyes. The line of mushrooms ended. To my shock, I'd blundered to the center of the island and found myself standing outside the gates of a castle.

I gazed up at the enormous structure. It towered over me, a black silhouette on the horizon. Light glowed through one of the windows in the upper floors. It was raining in earnest now.

Not waiting a moment longer, I pushed the gate. It swung open with a creak.

It was pouring.

I leaned my walking staff against a metal bench in the perfectly manicured garden, then grabbing my skirts, I ran for the castle door. As I rushed, lightning flashed. It created an odd illusion on the bushes and flowers around me. For a moment, they all seemed to glimmer like metal under the bright light.

My temples pounded. My stomach rolled. I raced through the heavy rain to the castle door.

Hoping whoever was at home would forgive me for letting myself in, I pushed open the castle door and crept inside.

The place was eerily silent.

"Hello?" I called. "Is anyone here?"

Breathing deeply and quickly, I realized the moment I stopped that I was not well.

I cast a glance toward a roaring fireplace nearby. A chair was seated before the hearth, a glass of something dark sitting beside the seat. I heard a strange clicking sound.

"Hello?" I called again, but this time, my head began to spin. I put my hands on my hips, trying to catch my breath. I closed my eyes. Everything was twirling.

Footsteps approached.

"I-I'm sorry I let myself in but..." I began then opened my eyes.

Standing before me was a massive automaton, its silver eyes staring coldly at me.

A nauseous feeling swept over me, and my head swam. Black spots danced before my eyes.

"Pardon me. I think I'm about to—"

Faint.

But the word was lost.

And so was I.

9
ARRESTED PERFECTION

"SHE'S COMING AROUND," A SOFT, FEMININE VOICE SAID. "Go tell him."

A pair of feet clomped heavily across the floor followed by the sound of a door opening and closing.

My head ached miserably, and I felt ill. I was lying in a warm and comfortable bed. I hated to open my eyes, but it wouldn't do to leave my hosts worrying about me after I fainted at the doorstep.

I opened my eyes and sat up slowly. I sat nestled in a massive poster bed. Sheer drapes had been drawn to mute the sunlight.

"Awake, mistress?" a soft voice called.

"Yes, thank you."

"You gave us a fright. You've been out for two days. You had a very nasty bump on the back of your head."

"I was shipwrecked."

"Indeed?"

"Are there any other survivors here? My father... We were separated in the wreck. Any of the other passengers or sailors wash ashore?"

"I have a pot of tea ready for you and a bite to eat," the woman said. "Let me bring your tray."

I sat up, adjusting myself in bed and coaching myself to be patient. I was a guest here, after all.

The woman pulled the drape aside. "You need to eat, mistress. You'll need to get your strength back. Mistress... My name is Missus Silver. Please, don't be frightened."

"Frightened?"

I stopped fluffing the pillows and looked up at the woman. My breath caught in my chest. Standing at my bedside holding a breakfast tray was an automaton. My mind flung back to the night I'd arrived and the hulking creature I'd seen in the hall. I hadn't hallucinated it. It was real, and so was the creature standing before me.

She looked every bit like a woman. She even had a mop of curls frozen in bronze, but her face had been made of porcelain. Where she should have had eyes, there were bright blue optics. Her mouth was jointed so it could open and close. She wore the gown of a maid with a long white apron and cap, but the dress was out of fashion, worn, and ripped at the seams. Her movements told me her entire body was machine.

I stared in wonderment.

"I know, I am a sight," she said then set the tray on my bed. "But at least you didn't scream."

"I...I... No, of course not."

"*I* didn't think you would. The others were not so sure. But I saw the necklace you're wearing, and I figured you might not be shocked."

"Necklace?" My eyes drifted down to my chest. I pulled out the leather cord I was wearing around my neck. On it were the windup keys for all of my beautiful devices which were now at the bottom of the sea. "The keys were for my creations."

"Creations?"

"Sculptures. Like music boxes. Clockwork. They were lost with the ship."

"I see. You know about such things then? Things like me?"

"Yes. My father and I are tinkers. Madame, is my father here? Any of the others? I'm sorry to press, but I need to look for my father. I need to send word to the mainland that the ship is lost. Please, where am I?"

"I'm afraid I can't answer any of those questions, dear. But the master will be by shortly."

"Master? Who is lord here?"

The automaton laughed a strange tinny sound. "He will tell you himself. Eat up, dear. Get your strength back," she said then turned and left, closing the door behind her.

I cast a glance around the room. The furnishings appeared to be in the style favored during Queen Anne's reign or older. I looked down at the gown I was wearing. The lace at the cuffs and along the neckline were beautifully made, but faded to yellow and very fragile. Everything in the room was exquisite but old.

I took a deep breath, steadied myself, then quickly drank the cup of tea—which tasted more herb than tea—and scarfed down the thick piece of bread. I had been starving. The flour used to make the bread had an odd tang I didn't recognize. It wasn't quite sourdough, but something similar. Once I'd eaten, I turned and set my feet on the floor.

I felt dizzy, my legs unsteady. Working slowly and carefully, I slipped out of bed and grabbed the dressing robe hanging nearby.

I crept to the door and listened. It was utterly silent.

Hearing nothing outside, I opened the door a crack and looked out.

My chamber was in a long, dimly lit hallway. Barefoot, I crept out of the room and down the hallway. The castle was truly wonderful. From paintings on the walls to fine sculptures in the alcoves to beautiful tapestries, the castle was luxurious and richly appointed. Whomever the lord of this little island was, he was a very wealthy man. It was, however, dim inside. I snatched a candelabra off a nearby table and went in search of…anything. Anyone. And most importantly, Papa.

As I glided down the halls, I checked each chamber. Room after room appeared to be empty, dusty, even. None of the bed chambers had been used in years. Climbing the steps to the third floor of the castle, I paused when I heard heavy footsteps in the hallway. I heard two male voices. Their cadence had that same metallic pitch as the maid. Was the lord a tinker? Had he fashioned these creations himself or purchased them with his obvious riches? If he was in the trade, perhaps he would know Papa. Maybe he was one of the members of the Rude Mechanicals, an elite society of tinkers in the realm. That would explain why he had such advanced mechs. We common tinkers had just begun to make some breakthroughs with more sophisticated automatons. But the maid had been truly extraordinary. Who had designed her?

The voices drew near.

I blew out the candle, set the candelabra aside, and slipped into a window alcove. The window was hung with a heavy green velvet drape that let in no light whatsoever. I hid in the darkness only peeking out from my hiding spot to watch as the two mechanical men made their way down the hall. Like the maid, they were dressed in servants' attire, although they both had the look more of Cavaliers than modern gentlemen. I waited as the footsteps retreated.

The dusty curtains made my nose burn. I stifled a cough. Turning, I took the quickest of glances out the window then paused.

My eyes narrowed as I focused on the flowers, the topiaries, the trees.

Outside, the sunlight shimmered blindingly on the garden.

Too blindingly.

And then, I understood why.

Turning, I rushed down the hallway to the stairs.

Grabbing the skirts of my dressing gown and robe, I ran down the steps. It wasn't until I reached the bottom steps that I realized how much my quick movements taxed me. I felt winded and woozy.

I heard heavy footsteps heading in my direction.

I flung open the front door and rushed out into the perfectly manicured garden. I raced along the prim garden path, past the distinctly box-shaped shrubs to the center of the garden. Turning around as I looked, I stared in disbelief at the beautiful rose arbors, the blooming dogwood trees, the bunches of wisteria, the twisting ivy, and the clipped topiaries in the shapes of swans and cupids. It was garden of refined taste. It was perfect in every way, each beautiful tree and blossom conforming to its training.

And every lovely bloom was arrested perfectly in place.

The entire garden was made of metal.

10
BITTERSWEET REUNIONS

"Mistress, what are you doing out here? Mistress, you must go back to your room at once," a male voice called.

I looked back toward the castle. One of the male servants, also made of clockwork, was ambling toward me. One of his two eyes, a yellow optic, had burnt out. His left leg moved with a screeching sound, not bending with fluidity. His hair, like the maid's, was arrested in silver. But his locks were long in the style favored in King Charles' day, as was his clothing. Didn't the lord of the house have the sense to re-dress his automatons? Perhaps the creations were merely that old.

"I… What is all this?" I asked the servant, waving toward the garden.

"The gardens. Now, if you please," the mechanical said, motioning back toward the house.

"Isabelle?" a distant voice called. I just barely heard my name on the wind. "Isabelle!"

My heart stopped beating.

I recognized the voice.

"Papa," I whispered. I scanned the castle. There, at the

very top of one of the castle turrets, I saw movement in a window. Papa was there.

"Papa," I yelled, waving.

I rushed past the automaton and back into the castle.

"Mistress! Mistress, wait," the mechanical called, but I ignored him.

I flung open the door to the castle and headed for the stairs.

"Mistress, where are you going? Mistress, wait," the maid called, but her voice box failed at the last words, the sound coming out garbled.

Ignoring the mechanicals, I raced up the steps.

"Papa," I yelled. "Papa, where are you?"

"Isabelle? Isabelle, I'm here."

I raced down a long hallway and up a short, winding flight of steps until I reached the door to the turret near the top of the castle.

"Papa?" I called, banging on the door. "Papa, are you there?"

"Isabelle? Oh, my sweet Isabelle. Thank God you are alive. I'm here," my father called.

Grabbing the door handle, I gave it a tug, but the door didn't open.

"It's locked, Isabelle."

"Locked? Why?"

"Because I locked it," a voice answered from further up the stairs. The voice was so dark and menacing that my heart skipped a beat.

"Papa," I whispered in a breath.

"Isabelle, it's all right. Don't be afraid."

"Why should she be afraid, old man? There's nothing monstrous here, except the monsters."

Heavy footsteps tromped slowly down the stairs toward me. I pressed myself against the door. My heart beat hard, the sound of it ringing in my ears. My breath quick, I felt woozy, and my stomach flopped, the tea and toast sloshing around. I felt like I was going to be sick.

The owner of the voice finally rounded the corner of the stairwell. First, I saw his heavy metal boots. He wore black hose, the cloth faded to an odd gray. My eyes drifted up. In addition to the hose, he had on a pale blue coat with a silk cravat. He had long hair, a square jaw, and a royal nose. His features were that of an aristocrat. But they were made entirely of metal.

He glared at me, his silver optics shining brightly through the narrowed metal eyelids. The optics turning, he regarded me carefully. He sneered then grabbed me by the wrist. Using a key attached to the tip of his finger, he unlocked the door.

Papa, who must have been standing close by, stepped back.

The mechanical pushed me into the room, entered behind me, then slammed the door closed behind us.

Holding my aching wrist, I rushed to Papa.

"Isabelle," Papa said, pulling me close to him.

The menacing mechanical glared at us. "Now, what am I supposed to do with the two of you?"

11
THE LORD AND THE AIRSHIP

I LOOKED FROM THE AUTOMATON TO THE WORKSHOP BEHIND me. To my surprise, suspended aloft was a tiny, one-person airship. The ship was not much larger or more advanced than a hot air balloon and nothing like the massive airships that flew in and out of the towers in London. The balloon had been painted periwinkle blue, though the color was much faded. A large red rose was painted on the side. Below the balloon hung a burner and a small gondola. I scanned the workroom. Tools were strewn everywhere. The place was, in fact, a hangar.

"Monster, my daughter is alive, and you didn't tell me?" Papa snapped at the mech.

I was shocked. I had never seen my father speak to anyone in anger. I then eyed Papa over. He was wearing a leather apron and had grease smeared across his face. Had he been working on the airship?

The mechanical laughed, his voice sounding tinny and hollow. "As if I am concerned with some peasant who washed up on my shore. And you, a thief, deserve nothing."

"Thief?" I asked. My father had never stolen anything in his life.

"The garden," Papa said. "You saw. The roses are all metal, all clockwork. One seemed to call to me. Foolish, I know. I picked it, thinking you would want to study its design. The castle seemed abandoned. No one was around. I figured there was no harm. But I was very wrong. I was locked in this room, made a prisoner because of a metal rose."

"No harm?" the lord said with a laugh. "You know nothing about harm. How dare you presume to pick my rose," the lord said with a snort. "A rose by any other name would still spell damnation for us all. Now, is your infernal device prepared? You and your daughter will board the ship and leave on it at once."

"You must be joking. This aircraft was designed to hold one person. It won't even lift with two aboard. As it is, the craft is an antique. If it flies at all, there is no guaranteeing how far it will go," Papa replied.

"Antique?" the lord said hotly. From within his metal body, I heard something click and whirl. The levers around the automaton's mouth moved his lips into the expression of a sneer. Once more, his eyes narrowed. "Then I guess one of you will just have to stay. You're both tinkers, I presume? My servants suggested as much. Fine. One of you will go, one of you will stay. My servants need repairs anyway."

"Stay? No," Papa said. "There must be another way. A ship? A rowboat? Does no one come here? This is a mad place, and you—a machine—may not lord over me or any living man."

At that, the automaton stepped menacingly toward my father.

Gasping, I stepped between them.

The lord eyed me skeptically then eased back.

"Mad? Indeed. This place is mad, as you would be in my place. No one comes here. Ever. And there is no other way off this island. Now, get your balloon ready, and send your daughter away from here, old man," he turned, his gears clicking as he looked at me. Once more, I saw his optics focus. He eyed me over, looking down at my chest.

In a fit of modesty, I clutched my dressing gown. But I quickly realized it wasn't me he was looking at—it was the windup keys.

"Where did you get those?" he snapped, reaching out for the keys.

I clutched my hand around them. "They're mine. They are the keys to my creations."

"Your creations? What creations?"

"Music boxes. Nothing more. They're at the bottom of the sea. Go have a look."

The mechanical looked from the keys back to my face. His eyes narrowed once more then he turned and stomped to the door. "I will give you a moment to say goodbye. Prepare that ship. One of the two of you will be getting on. Decide. Now," he said then slammed the door behind him.

12
FAREWELL

"PAPA," I WHISPERED, LOOKING UP AT MY FATHER.

My father planted kisses on my forehead and cheeks. "Isabelle, are you all right? What happened to you? Where have you been?"

"I was injured in the shipwreck, a blow to the head. I found my way here but fainted. I have been asleep in a chamber below. I had no idea you were here. And you? How did you find this place?"

"Quite by chance, I stumbled upon the castle after I floated to shore on a barrel. I found a path leading here. I hoped to get help, a search party—men, horses, dogs—to find you and the others. But when I picked the rose, the lord—or so he fashions himself—appeared and called me a thief. I fear what he might have done if I hadn't I explained I was a tinker and that I was only curious. He brought me here. I've been locked in the workshop ever since. He's been very anxious to be rid of me."

I chuckled lightly, trying to ease Papa. "Certainly no rescue party to be had at this castle."

"The lord *does* have a dog."

"Is it…"

Papa nodded.

"I don't understand. How did such advanced mechanicals come to be here? From their clothing, they date back a century or more."

"Look," Papa said, motioning to the room behind him. "This workshop is quite advanced, but the tools are all very old. The airship is one of the first ever built. This particular ship was designed by Archibald Boatswain himself," he said, referring to the master tinker who'd invented the first airships and Tinker's Tower, which had been a gift from the London Tinkers Society to Queen Anne.

I stared up at the airship. Such machines had taken my mother from me and changed the course of my father's life. Would we never be rid of them? My voice trembling, I said, "Papa, you must be the one to go. Fly the ship to the mainland then come back and get me. You will be able to better note the landscape as you go and rediscover the island. And you know these machines. I do not."

"Isabelle, I cannot possibly leave you here with this monstrous creature. He's no man. He's all machine, and I fear his ethics circuitry is incomplete or damaged. He truly thinks he is the lord of this castle. The other mechs treat him as such, and he is as haughty as any blueblood I've ever met. He cannot be trusted. We must find another way off the island."

"I have seen none. Have you?"

Papa shook his head.

"We cannot take the airship together?" I asked.

Papa stiffened. "I would not risk you in an airship, Isabelle. You know that. And this ship will not hold us both."

"No chance at all, the risk aside?"

Papa waved for me to follow him. We climbed the ladder to the platform outside the airship. The workshop had a very high ceiling, and as I looked upward, I saw that the roof was connected to a series of levers which opened it. The balloon burner on the airship had already been lit. I frowned. Early ships such as these were unwieldy to steer and easily tossed about by the wind. Only a steady, practiced hand could fly one. And flying one over the sea where the winds were more likely to pitch a person about was even riskier. Papa had to go. He had to. If one of us could escape, he had the better chance of navigating the ship and finding me once more.

"Look," Papa said, motioning to the small, slender gondola. As I looked inside, I understood. The gears, levers, all of the cockpit had been designed to hold one person only. The airship could not carry two.

"I cannot drive it. Please, Papa. Please. Return to England then come for me," I said, feeling tears prick the corners of my eyes.

My father stood staring at the ship.

"Isabelle, you know I swore I would never—"

The door to the chamber opened once more. The lord went to the side of the room, where he activated a lever. A pulley on the wall shifted, and slowly, the roof above the turret opened.

A soft spring breeze wafted in from outside. I closed my eyes, feeling the wind and sunlight on my cheeks.

"Isabelle," my father said, his voice filled with anguish.

I turned and looked at him. "I have faith in you, Papa. I know you are frightened, but you can do this. Do this to save us both. Go. I know you will find me again," I said then leaned in and whispered, "Advanced or not, these mechs are very old, and my hands are very nimble. It will take almost nothing to deactivate them. If things become uncomfortable, I will simply turn them off."

My father exhaled in relief then nodded.

"Have you decided?" the lord called.

"I shall go," Papa said.

"Then go. And do not seek to return to this place."

Papa gave me a knowing glance then pulled me into an embrace.

"I love you, Papa," I whispered.

"I love you too. Be careful. Be safe."

I nodded, kissing my father on the cheek once more, then stepped back.

Reluctantly, my father climbed into the cockpit.

I climbed back down the ladder. Unlocking the brakes on the wooden platform, I rolled it away while the lord unlocked the clamps holding the airship in place.

"Isabelle?"

"Papa! I love you, Papa. Be safe."

When the lord released the last clamp, the airship began to rise.

Biting the inside of my cheek, I watched as the airship lifted away from the tower, up and out of sight, taking Papa along with it. Tears threatened, but I fought them back. I would not let this beastly creature see me cry, not that it understood emotion anyway.

The mech activated the lever once more, closing the roof of the turret again.

"You're very brave to stay in your father's place," the lord said.

"Brave? He is my father. Of course I would suffer in his place."

The lord stiffened and stood in a formal, rigid posture. "Suffer?" he said with a sniff. "Oh no. You will not suffer at my hands. You might be a simple tinker, not a lady, but you are my guest here. Now, my servants tell me you are unwell. Is that so? You should return to your room and rest."

"Oh. Aren't you grand telling me to rest after everything you've done," I said then turned to leave.

The mech stepped in front of the door, blocking my path. He eyed me carefully, optics turning, metallic eyelids narrowing. He looked at my hand where I held my wrist against my chest.

I had hidden the bruise from Papa, but when the metallic monster had grabbed me, pushing me into the room, his grip had been tight. My wrist ached and was turning purple.

"What's wrong with your arm?" the lord asked.

I laughed. "What was it you said? I won't suffer at your hands? Why don't you have a look at your handiwork?" I said, shoving my arm out so he could see. The skin around my wrist was red and purple and swelling visibly. "Beastly creature," I said hotly then dodged around him and headed back down the stairs.

"Miss… Miss Hawking, isn't it? Miss Hawking, it was an accident. I don't know the strength of this machine," the lord said.

Furious, frightened, sad, and confused, I raced back to the bedchamber and slammed the door closed behind me.

My father was gone.

And I was left alone with a metallic beast.

13
THE GREAT ESCAPE

MISSUS SILVER CAME TO MY DOOR TWICE TO TRY TO persuade me to come out, but I didn't answer. From somewhere deeper in the castle, I heard the loud grumblings of the lord. I stared out the window of the castle. From my chamber, I could see the garden below, its metal and clockwork flowers. But beyond that, I saw the island where thick trees grew.

I might have been trapped in this terrible place until Papa returned, but that didn't mean I had to stay locked in my chamber. I was no Rapunzel.

I opened up the wardrobe to discover several freshly laundered dresses had been left for me. They were all very old and far too elaborate for my taste. I was relieved to spot my simple traveling gown. I slipped it and my boots back on then, creeping quietly, I went to the door.

I heard voices, but they were not close by.

Tiptoeing quickly and carefully, I headed downstairs.

My head still ached. It was a miracle I had not drowned.

I crept across the main foyer. I could hear the lord and one of his attendants in a room off the great hall. The door was open just a crack. I crept to the door and peered within.

"I am sorry, my lord. My hand is not as steady as it used to be," the attendant was saying.

The lord and his servant were sitting at the end of a long dining room table in a great hall. He had removed his jacket and rolled up the sleeve of his shirt. His arm lay on the table, the metal casing open. I could just make out the clockwork mechanisms inside the arm. I pressed forward a little for a better look.

"Do your best. That is all any of us can do," the lord said.

The attendant set his tools aside then slid a crystal goblet toward his master. "Try that," he said.

The lord attempted to pick up the cup, but it shattered in his grasp. The sound of broken glass echoed throughout the hall. The lord sighed.

"Widdershins, Mister Flint," the lord said, brushing the broken goblet aside. "It's worse than before. The grip must be lessened, not increased. I don't want any more...miscalculations."

"Sorry, my lord. Very sorry," the servant said then picked up his tools again.

I winced as I watched, my fingers twitching as the servant applied a bricklayer's delicacy to a job that required a surgeon's precision. Once again, the servant worked on the lord's hand. Satisfied, he pushed another cup toward his master.

"Try this, my lord," he said.

The lord of the castle moved to pick up his cup, but when his fingers flexed, they were far too soft, and the cup slipped from his grasp, crashing to the floor and splintering into a million glistening pieces.

"Oh, my lord. I am so s-s-s-o-rr-rr-yyy," the servant said, his voice box fading at the end. The servant went quiet and became still, frozen mid-gesture.

The lord sighed, if such a thing was possible, then reached into his coat pocket. From within, he pulled out a small metal device. At first, I couldn't see what it was. He unbuttoned the servant's old coat and shirt and pushed it aside to show a metal compartment, and within it a keyhole, on the automaton's back. The lord slipped in a windup key and turning the device, which made an audible click, he wound the mech.

When he removed the key, the servant activated once more.

"...sorry. It is difficult to be precise. I say, my lord, what happened?" the servant asked, looking down at his shirt which the lord was rebuttoning with care that seemed out of line with his temperament.

"You wound down, Mister Flint," the lord answered simply.

"Happening more and more these days," the servant said. "To all of us."

"Yes."

"And you, my lord? Any...luck?"

"Don't think of it."

"The girl—Miss Hawking—is a tinker like her father. Did you see? She's wearing—"

"I saw. Forget it. They're nothing."

"But the girl—"

"I said, don't think of it. Now, let's begin again," the lord said, extending his arm once more.

I leaned back. No wonder my windup keys had gotten the attention of the automatons. They needed them for their very survival. Such a strange and ill-omened place. I took a deep breath, quickly tiptoed to the front door, then slowly and quietly slipped outside.

A soft breeze whipped across the garden. While the trees beyond the walls waved, the garden itself, however, was arrested in its beauty. Turning down a garden path, I walked through the metallic sculptures. I had never seen artwork like this before. Every blossom, every leaf, was made of metal. They were all so perfectly designed. I went to examine a flowering topiary meant to look like gardenia. I was surprised when a butterfly with gossamer silver wings rose from the sculpture and fluttered off. At first, I thought the creature only silvery, but I followed the shimmering creation to its next landing point, a clockwork rose. It rested there, its wings wagging as it adjusted its clockwork antennas.

I gasped as I looked at the intricacy of the creation. How had it been designed with such small gears?

The blossom on which the silver butterfly had landed slowly opened. It was very similar to my own sculpture, *Love's Bloom*, which featured a rose arbor and the lovers. As this rose opened, however, I was unable to see the levers operating the petals. It was perfectly designed.

I turned and looked around the grounds.

I loved art. I loved capturing the beauty of nature in clock-work. The grounds were one massive sculpture. My own work, which even the most senior in the London Tinker's Society considered advanced, dwarfed in comparison. Why had someone created this? And how?

From beyond the wall behind me, I heard a soft giggle. The wind blew, and the leaves on the living trees on the other side of the wall wagged in the breeze. Once more, I heard the sound of bells and smelled the sweet perfume of new leaves and loamy earth.

I looked back at the castle. I saw movement through the dining room window and the glint of metal. No one was going to force me back inside. I glared at the castle then turned and followed the path to the gate. It was not the same one through which I'd entered before. Here, there was a small station for a gatekeeper, and the entryway was far more elaborate. Massive letter Ls trimmed the structure. This must have been the formal entrance. That meant that the path leading toward the water must have reached a dock. I eyed the guard post. The station was empty. I pushed the ornate gate open just enough to slip out. And I was glad I did so, because a moment later, I heard one of the lord's clockwork attendants calling my name.

I glared back at the castle.

Grabbing the skirts of my dress, I rushed down the overgrown cart path until the garden was out of sight. But even then, I heard someone open the gate behind me. I cast a glance all around. There was no way I was going back anytime soon. I needed to get off this path. I looked into the woods. Everywhere looked the same: thick, deep, dark forest. Well, it was an island. There was no getting lost. At some point, I'd eventually find the beach. Turning off the path, I fled into the woods.

14
IN THE GREEN

I STOPPED RUNNING WHEN I RAN OUT OF BREATH. MY LUNGS burned, and my head ached. Sitting down on a rock, I inhaled deeply and fought off the black spots before my eyes. My head felt dizzy once more. Reason suggested that I should probably be still in bed. But reason also suggested that I was trapped on an island where automaton sentinels ruled—including a mech who thought he was a lord. I wasn't sure who had left the clanking menace behind, but someone needed to work on his ethics circuits. I rubbed the bruise on my arm then stared into the forest.

Everything was so green. Shades ranging from deep emerald green to bright chartreuse colored the canvas. Ahead of me was an opening in the canopy. A single standing stone stood there, slants of light shining down on it from above. Around it, a bed of new ferns grew, their soft fingers uncurling in the sunlight. The sunlight shimmered onto the stone.

Rising, I went to inspect the ancient structure. It was taller than myself by at least another two feet. On it had been carved many Celtic symbols and knots. I spotted a mirror and comb, a horse, a horned man, ravens, and wolves. Along the edge of the stone were the ancient Ogham symbols. I traced the ancient language, running my finger over the rough stone. I could not stand the idea that there was something to be learned here, something to be read, and I simply could not read it.

The wind blew once more, and once again, I heard voices on the wind. That overwhelming feeling that I was not alone swept over me.

"Hello?" I whispered, my skin rising to gooseflesh. My very bones felt the presence of something else in the woods with me.

But there was nothing.

I did notice, however, that the stone on which I was sitting had also been carved with a face, much like the stone I'd found not far from the beach.

"Sorry, ancient one," I said, rising. "How very rude of me."

The wind gusted. The canopy overhead shifted, and I spotted a lush area in the forest where forget-me-nots covered the forest floor. I walked toward the enchanting scene. Tomorrow, I would find something to write with—first I had to see what condition my journal was in—and then I'd come back to this place. To pass the time, I'd note the Ogham inscriptions, copy the designs on the stones. Something told me it would be awhile before I felt like tinkering clockwork devices again. In the meantime, however, the mystery of the stones intrigued me. When Papa returned—and he would return, I had no doubt— I would find a key to the Ogham language and uncover the message.

The little patch of flowers, wild and full of color, was almost more than I could stand. The cheery blue faces, the center of the flowers yellow, colored the forest floor like they'd been painted by Mother Nature. I saw hues of pink and purple amongst the tiny flowers, the imperfections of nature which only made the scene more perfect. I sat down amongst the flowers. Everywhere I looked, I saw blue.

I laughed.

How perfectly natural and disorganized the flowers were. How unlike the castle garden. How sweet and innocent and natural.

I laughed again.

Hard.

Until I cried.

"Hurry, Papa," I whispered, brushing hot tears off my cheeks.

The wind blew once more. The soft breeze ruffled my hair and caressed my cheek as if to comfort me.

Sighing, I rose. I wanted to pick a bouquet of the flowers, but they were far too perfect as they were. I would not disturb the natural beauty of the place. Rising, I returned to the cart path once more. This time, I followed it. The trail led to the shore, but as I walked, I spotted a side road. Here, the track had been worn down by carts, trees cleared to force a path through the woods. Curious, I followed the trail. Alongside this lane, I saw where some of the massive oak trees had been cut, but their timbers lay fallen on the forest floor. Where one enormous oak had been felled, I spied a standing stone crushed underneath. My heart seized to see the ancient monolith so mistreated. I moved further along until I approached a hill. Before it, the land had been cleared. A ramshackle building, walls collapsed, and the roof caved in, sat nearby. Pulley systems lay broken on the ground. Carts, their wheels rusted, sat forgotten. There was an entrance to the hill, a crack in the rocks that looked, at least at first glance, like a cave. But when I studied it more closely, eyeing the fallen carts and tools lying around the entrance, I realized it was, in fact, a mine. Rail lines had been worked into the ground and led into the narrow cave. A row of rail carts lay forgotten to the side.

The woods here were very still, very silent.

I approached the entrance to the mine and looked inside.

The mine was, in fact, a cave. Someone had built the mine shaft into the natural formation. As I looked around the entrance of the cave, I saw Celtic symbols and Ogham engraved into the cave opening.

A breeze blew from within the cave. It smelled of mud and minerals. The denseness of it made my heart feel heavy. No. Not heavy. Something here felt…sad. Desperately sad.

I stepped back.

I turned around and looked at all the ruins. How unnatural, how unclean all the axes and rail lines and chains and ropes were. They marred the natural beauty of this place. Suddenly feeling ill at ease, I turned and rushed back into the forest, back into the green spaces, back where I could breathe free again. But most of all, I needed to escape the terrible foreboding that had shaken me to my core.

15
SURELY HE HAS A SCREW LOOSE

RELUCTANTLY, I RETURNED TO THE CASTLE. AS I WALKED, I thought about the lord. He'd asked his servant to correct the grip on the hand that had bruised my arm. What had he said when I'd confronted him: *"I don't know the strength of this machine."* That was an odd way to put it. From what I could see, the repair of his arm could be made easily. I had the tools in my satchel, and it would only take a moment. Maybe I would offer to do the repair. Perhaps it would buy me some goodwill in the castle until Papa returned.

When I reached the door to the castle, it was already growing dark. The sun burned low on the horizon. Shades of orange, red, and pink illuminated the skyline and made the metal garden shimmer as the materials reflected the haze. How odd that the metals did not corrode under the elements. Bronze always faded to green and—

The door to the castle opened with a heave.

"Where did you go? Where have you been?" someone demanded.

I turned to find the lord standing there staring menacingly at me. In the dimming light, his gray optics glowed ominously.

"I…I was just——"

"Never leave the grounds again. Do you understand? Do not go beyond the walls of the garden," he shouted, his voice box shrill and dark. He took a few steps toward me, his heavy feet clanging intimidatingly.

I felt my ire rise. I pulled myself up to my full height and stomped to him. "Or what?" I asked sharply, coming face to face with him. "You'll rough me about again? Your ethics circuits are rusted, you tired old mechanical." Judging that he would not be able to swivel in time, I ducked and dashed past him into the castle. I slammed the door behind me. Grabbing my skirts, I sprinted up the steps.

The door opened once more.

"Miss Hawking, come back here. You *will* allow me to explain," he called commandingly from behind me.

"I will do nothing. You are not my lord. I want no explanations from you. Go rust somewhere," I said then rushed back up the steps. I raced back to my bedchamber and closed and locked the door behind me.

I heard voices in the hall below. Missus Silver and Mister Flint were talking to the lord, whose tone of voice seemed to vacillate from furious to capitulating.

And to think, I'd considered helping the metallic menace. Beastly creature. I'd think about him no more. From now on, I'd occupy my time noting down the designs in the clockwork garden and deciphering the Ogham written on the stones. I lifted my satchel. It was dry, but I worried about the contents.

There was a knock at the door.

"Go away," I called, instantly feeling like an impetuous child.

"Miss Hawking," the lord called from the other side of the door. "You must allow me to explain. Perhaps… Perhaps you would dine with me tonight."

I set my bag down and went to the door.

I opened it with such sudden ferocity that he stepped back.

"Dine with you? You're mad. What, shall I watch you sup on oil and bolts? Leave me alone. When my father returns, I shall leave this place at once and think on you no more," I said then slammed the door again.

"Do you really think your father is going to come back? Do you really think he will ever be able to find this place again? You are the one who's mad, Miss Hawking. No living person has set foot in this place in more than a hundred years. Your father will never find you again. You are trapped here, just like the rest of us," the lord snarled then stomped back down the hall.

I stared at the door. That wasn't possible. What he was saying wasn't true. Papa would find me. He would return. I had no doubt. I frowned at the door. Meddlesome mech. What did he know? Someone had designed him to make him think himself a nobleman. That crumbling antique! He had no idea the world outside of this place had changed. Maybe he'd been trapped here more than a hundred years, but I wouldn't be. Papa was the brightest tinker in London and had the best minds at his disposal. He would return soon.

I sat down again at the desk and pulled my books out of my satchel. They had gotten waterlogged but had since dried. The book on Hero of Alexandria was destroyed. The ink on the pages had washed to nothing, the designs mere shadows. The pages were so glued together that any effort to lift them apart would cause them to tear. Pity. Mister Walpole's book on goblins, to my surprise, was intact. In fact, the pages barely curled at all, and there'd been no damage to the ink. A goblin spell must have kept it safe, surely. The book on mystical artifacts had taken some damage, but the majority of the book was still intact. My journal had survived, but much of the new ink had bled and faded, including the sketch I'd made on the ill-fated *Prospero*.

I set out my tools, pens, and the mirror Elyse Murray had given me. I slid down into my seat and stared at the books. My stomach growled hungrily.

Sighing, I tipped my head back and closed my eyes.

Papa would find me, and before I knew it, I would be back in London again fending off Gerard LeBoeuf and fashioning my own designs, a prospect that, despite my unending love for the trade, suddenly felt much less appealing.

16
BE OUR GUEST

I HAD FALLEN ASLEEP, MY HEAD RESTING ON MY ARMS AT MY desk, when there was a knock on the door.

"Miss Hawking," Missus Silver called.

I sat up with a yawn. My head ached, my stomach knotted with hunger.

"Yes?"

The door opened, the automaton appearing at the door with a candelabra in her hand. She smiled, an odd sort of expression on her face. "Miss, you must be starving. The lord is…has retired. Will you come eat, my dear? Missus Smith, our cook, has prepared you something to eat in the dining room."

Frowning, I considered it. The last thing I wanted to do was mix with the lord and his servants, but if he had retired, then there would be no harm. In that moment, I realized my stomach was overruling my wits, which was often the case. But I was ravenous.

"Very well," I said then followed Missus Silver.

We walked in silence down the long hall and stairwell to the formal dining room. A long table stretched out before me. The chandelier overhead had been lit as well as the candelabras on the table. At one end of the table, a meal sat waiting under a gold dome.

"Mistress," the male automaton said. He pulled out my chair. "I am Mister Flint. Please, have a seat."

I slipped into the chair.

"Your dinner is served," he said, removing the golden dome.

Underneath was a beautifully prepared meal. A rosy red lobster, delicate mushrooms in sauce, and delicious baked bread awaited. I stared down at the feast then at the gold-plated flatware, including a golden cup and saucer. The footman brought wine and poured me a goblet. The wine cup was made of crystal and trimmed with gold filigree. Such expensive items had a royal flair. I was suddenly reminded of my clockwork sculpture of the dining table with the flatware that wove and danced in tune. Of course, now it was at the bottom of the sea.

"I am sorry, mistress, that the offerings are meager, and we cannot provide the proper courses. We, as you can guess, do not need such replenishment anymore and have to make do with what the island provides."

"No, no," I said. "This is beautiful, and it smells divine."

"Then please, eat. You are our guest here."

"I wish your lord—as he fashions himself—felt the same way," I said as I sipped the wine. The vintage had a mellow, fruity flavor.

"Fashions? No. He is our lord. That is certain. He has always come across as the brooding sort, but time has darkened him, I'm afraid."

"Darkened him?"

Missus Silver turned toward the footman, and a series of distinct clicks emerged from her chest.

"Yes, Missus Silver, you're quite right," Mister Flint said

then bowed to me. "I'll return in a time with a dessert for you, mistress."

"Thank you," I said, eyeing Missus Silver skeptically. What had she signaled to Mister Flint? I wanted to puzzle it out, but my stomach rumbled. I lifted my fork and took a bite of the mushrooms. They were heavenly. They'd been fire-roasted with fresh herbs. The flavors melted on my tongue.

I had eaten lobster a few times before, Papa and I laughing as we made a mess of the entire dining room, much to Martin's bemused horror. Trying to be a bit more refined—well, as much as possible—I worked on removing the lobster tail. I still failed in my feminine duties when a bit of lobster went flying across the dining room. I was suddenly very glad the lord was not there to give me a metallic sneer.

"Lost a bite," Missus Silver said with mirth in her voice.

"It's tough to eat this properly," I said with a smile.

"Yes. I know. Miss Hawking, I understand you were in the garden today."

I nodded, my mouth full of bread. I lifted a finger, asking her for a moment, took a sip of the wine then swallowed. "It's a lovely and unexpected place. Quite enchanting, really. The architect must have been a tinker of rare talent."

"Rare talent? Yes, well, that is one way of putting it. But you should have seen it long ago," she said with a sad sigh. "It was the most heavenly place in the world."

I raised an eyebrow at her. "Indeed? It's held up remarkably well in the weather. You all must take excellent care of it. I haven't seen even a spot of rust."

"We look after it like we do all things here."

I eyed the mech. While I knew her programming was all analytic machine, ethics boards, and an aether core, there was something very human about her manner. Sadness hung heavily on her. Surely I was reading more into her than was there. I broke off a bit of bread then looked out the window. It was dark outside. The sky was absolutely full of stars.

"The forest beyond these walls," I said, motioning, "is magical beyond anything I have ever seen. And, I think, has some history."

"Oh, yes. This small island was sister to Ynys Dywyll, as it was once called."

"Ynys Dywyll—the Isle of Anglesey?"

The mech nodded. "You've been outside the walls. Perhaps you saw the stone rings and standing stones?"

"I did," I said then cracked open the lobster claw. Considering there was no one around other than Missus Silver, I set aside my golden fork and took a bite. Much easier. Working with my hands, I began to dismantle the crustacean.

"Our lord once told me that back in the ancient times when the Romans invaded, they destroyed the Druids' shrines and decimated Anglesey. Those who survived retreated to this island."

"Druids? Well, that would explain the standing stones. And in the woods, I'd swear I felt something magical."

"The woods here have many eyes and lots of memories."

"I hope to record those memories. Tomorrow, I shall return to the forest and make a note of the stones. Do you have a map of the island? Perhaps if I make a grid, I can ensure I don't miss any of the menhirs. I'd like to sketch the stones and record the Ogham script thereon."

"The forest is not safe, Miss Hawking. You should not roam outside the castle gates again."

"Why not? What's out there?"

The automaton clicked. "Wolves."

I turned and looked at her. "Wolves? On an island?"

Even the most sophisticated mech cannot replicate human emotion with any precision, but at that moment, I could very clearly see that Missus Silver was lying.

"Yes," she replied with false certainty. "Large, dangerous wolves. You must stay inside the walls. You may feel free to use the garden as much as you like, but you cannot leave the safety of the grounds. Do you understand?"

I frowned but said nothing more. Clearly, this was the lord's message that she was delivering. Why was he so insistent I stay inside the castle walls?

Missus Silver busied herself with pouring more wine. If I had hadn't known better, I would have thought it a nervous distraction. But now my curiosity was piqued. How much did the mech actually know?

"I thought, perhaps, you were concerned I would get hurt amongst the old mining equipment," I said leadingly.

Missus Silver froze. She set down the wine bottle then turned to look at me. Her optics narrowed. A series of clicks rattled in her chest. "You…found the mine?"

I nodded.

"Miss Hawking, that place is very, very dangerous. I implore you, do not return there."

"I found the place quite odd. It really didn't seem like a mine at all. The opening to the cavern had carvings all around it just like on the standing stones. I noted Celtic designs and Ogham as well."

"Miss Hawking," Missus Silver said. Her voice box boomed so loudly that it echoed down the hallway, which made the feedback from her voicebox screech. From somewhere within her body, I heard very loud ticking increasing rapidly. She set her hand on my arm. "Please, mistress. Please. For all our sakes, don't go there again."

"Why not? Missus Silver, what's wrong?"

"Please. Please. You cannot. You must not. Please, don't go there again. You must promise not to go there again."

"Missus Silver?" The ticking inside the machine was growing even louder, and the automaton's optics brightened.

"Promise, Miss Hawking. Promise. Promise?"

"Missus Silver, what's happening?" I asked, standing. The mech's eyes were flashing as her chest continued to click and rattle.

"Please, please, please, pleeeeease, ppplllleeasssee," she repeated, the ticking growing louder and louder until there was a terrible pop.

I smelled a whiff of sulfur then Missus Silver's eyes went dim. She slumped over, bending at the waist.

"Oh damn," I whispered.

17
ALMOST KIND

Moving carefully, I lowered Missus Silver into a seat at the table. I studied her optics. There was still light flickering at the very back, but she had clearly damaged some of her circuitry. Looking carefully, I checked her body for signs of damage. Her back felt hot, and I saw a bit of scorching on the back of her shirt.

"Missus Silver, please excuse me," I said then began to undo the small buttons on the back of her shirt. Sure enough, there was a panel between her shoulder blades from which I smelled sulfur and felt the heat.

Grabbing a knife to pop open the back panel, I looked at the circuitry inside.

"Madame!" Mister Flint said, reappearing in the dining room. "What's happening?"

"I believe Missus Silver overheated. Do you have a toolkit?" I asked, knowing full well I had seen the mech with the tools earlier that day.

The mech nodded then went to the cabinet at the side of the room. From within, he brought out the large wooden cabinet I had seen earlier that day. He set it on the table.

I pushed my hair away from my face then squinted at the small clockwork devices inside Missus Silver. I suddenly wished I had my magnifying goggles.

"Bring some light," I said.

Mister Flint lifted a candelabra.

"Ah. There it is," I said, seeing where a cog had come loose. I dug into the toolbox and grabbed the smallest pair of pliers I could find. Working slowly, I removed the broken pieces then set them aside. Grabbing a repair piece from the toolbox, I started to set a replacement cog in place.

Heavy footsteps thundered toward the dining room.

"What's happening here?" the lord complained as he strode across the room.

"Missus Silver broke down. Miss Hawking is making the repair," Mister Flint answered.

"What? How dare you work on her without my permission?"

"Why don't you yell at me *after* I restore Missus Silver?" I snapped. "Now, be quiet so I can concentrate."

I heard a series of clicks pass between the lord and his servant, but no one spoke another word.

Using the tiny tools, I fixed the cog in place.

Exhaling, I stepped back. "Done. Now, how do you reanimate her?"

The lord pulled out his windup key, but the grip on his fingers betrayed him, and he dropped it. When he bent to retrieve it, I noticed he used the hand opposite the one his servant had attempted to repair.

The lord slipped a windup key into a keyhole right above the panel on Missus Silver's back. He turned the key, rewinding Missus Silver, then pulled the key out slowly.

Missus Silver sat erect. At first, her words came out garbled then she stood and said very distinctly, "No, Miss Hawking. Please. Please don't go there again."

Everyone in the room stilled.

Missus Silver turned and looked around. "Oh dear! I do believe I malfunctioned."

"One moment," I told her then replaced the panel. The lord and Mister Flint looked away as I buttoned up Missus Silver's shirt. "There you are, Missus Silver."

"Miss Hawking, thank you so much. Yes, my analytics in that sector are working much better now."

"It's the least I can do. I'm sorry our previous conversation upset—"

"Think nothing of it," she said, cutting me off. Clearly, she did not want to return to the topic with the lord present.

The lord narrowed his eyes, looking from me to Missus Silver. He frowned then said, "Thank you for fixing her. I believe we interrupted your dinner. Please sit. Enjoy your meal," he said, pulling out my chair for me.

Eyeing him warily, I returned to my seat.

The lord nodded to his servants, who then disappeared. Missus Silver and Mister Flint clicked to one another as they went.

He took a seat nearby. "May I ask what you were discussing with Missus Silver when she became so upset?"

I lifted the glass of wine and sat back in my seat. I was not in the mood for another scolding. "The woods."

The lord looked carefully at me. "The woods here are dangerous."

"So I'm told. There are giant, ferocious wolves out there, from what I heard."

The lord's metal mouth moved into an expression like a smirk. "Wolves? Did she think you would believe her?"

I smiled softly, surprised by his candor. "Yes, I think so."

He smiled. "There are no wolves, as you no doubt already guessed, but the forest is not safe."

"I mentioned to Missus Silver that I hoped to record some

information on the standing stones I saw. I was hoping to sketch the designs and note down the Ogham writing."

"Can you read the language?"

"Not yet. Perhaps if I had a key. But with a little time, key or no, one can decipher the language."

"How?"

"Patterns, of course."

"Patterns," he repeated. "And if you study the patterns, you may be able to read the stones?"

"Yes."

The lord sat back in his seat and stroked his chin where his pointed pickdevant beard in the Rococo style was arrested in metal.

"The western side of the island can be explored without excessive risk. There are a number of stones west of the castle. You may explore the western side of the island, but no further. Do not pass the castle to the east. Do you understand?"

I looked at him. I most certainly did not understand, but with my freedom hanging so tantalizingly in front of me, I didn't dare say so. "Yes," I replied simply.

He nodded. "Good. Ah," he said, reaching for the bottle of wine. "I see they selected you a nice vintage."

But when he grabbed the bottle, his grasp was loose and the bottle tipped.

Moving quickly, I grabbed it before it fell over.

When I did so, the lord stared at my bruised wrist.

"Thank you. I... The controls on my left arm are problematic. I injured the arm, and it hasn't been right since. Miss Hawking, I really do apologize for what happened. I was taken aback by the unexpected appearance of you and your father on my island. In my alarm, I believe I was rough in tone and became careless regarding the crudeness of my mechanics. It is so very far beneath me and not in my character to injure you. Please, I hope you will forgive me."

I eyed him skeptically. Automatons were not supposed to be able to lie or deceive, but Missus Silver had just invented giant wolves. Could I trust this self-fashioned mechanical lord? He did seem sincere. Given what I had observed, it was an accident. It didn't do to be angry with a machine.

"If you would like, it would be very easy for me to make the adjustment to your grip. As you have seen, I am an adept tinker."

The lord considered. "Very well."

I rose from my seat, grabbed the toolkit, then sat closer to the lord. I tried not to think about the fact that my lobster was cold and that I had an entire mini loaf of bread still waiting for me, nor the fact that I was still hungry. At that moment, it felt far more important to help. In fact, it felt good. It felt right. The lord didn't want to hurt anyone. There was honor in that.

The lord rolled up his sleeve and lay his arm on the table. Moving carefully, he opened the metal covering on his inner arm to reveal the clockwork devices inside.

I inhaled deeply, fighting off the wooziness too much wine on an empty stomach had caused, then stared at the mechanisms.

"Wiggle your fingers, please," I said, watching devices work.

I nodded then handed the lord my golden teacup. "If you drop it, it won't chip," I said with a soft smile. "Please take it by the handle."

He did as I asked, all the while watching me as I studied him. His latch around the handle on the cup was far too loose.

"Now grip the cup around its girth and lift it."

When he did so, the cup slipped from his fingers and fell to the table. The thumb and forefinger were in better shape than the rest of the hand.

Nodding, I gently lowered his arm and looked within. To my surprise, the metal was as warm as flesh.

Ignoring the unexpected sensation, I eyed the configuration then spotted the problem. "Ah, there we are," I said.

Fishing around in Mister Flint's toolbox for a screwdriver, plyers, and torque wrench, I finally found everything I needed. I leaned over his arm and studied the gears. I lifted the pliers but paused for a moment.

"This may be uncomfortable," I said, looking up at him as he studied me. "Is it possible for you to shut down until I'm done? If you give me your windup key, I can restart you thereafter."

The lord snorted, but not rudely. "I wish that were possible, Miss Hawking. I will have to stay alert."

"Very well," I said then moved a candelabra close to us so I could see better. Moving delicately, I adjusted the mechanics inside. It took some time to get them all settled. I could feel the lord's optics on me, watching me closely. I steadied my breath and tried to ignore him, focusing on my task. The clockwork mechanisms inside were really no more complicated than the sculpture I'd done of the birds on the branch. In no time, I had it. Setting the tools aside, I sat back. "Move your fingers, please."

He did as I asked. The fingers worked in unison.

Picking up the cup once again, I set it before him. "The handle, to start."

He nodded then lifted the cup. I watched as his fingers worked. They were steady, firm, and aligned.

"Now grasp it."

Once more, he grasped the cup. This time, he didn't drop it.

"Hold. Like this," I said, setting my arm on my elbow, my hand extended.

Moving my chair closer to the lord, I carefully examined the grip of his fingers on the cup. It held in place without denting. His grip was neither too firm nor too soft. As I leaned to look, I heard a slightly audible tick coming from his chest that sounded like the beat of a heart.

He made a noise as if he was clearing his throat then shifted a little away from me.

Nodding, I pulled back. "I think we have it there. How does it feel to you?"

He set the cup down then lifted it again. "Very good. Thank you, Miss Hawking. The hand has given me trouble for some years. None of us had the skill to fix it."

I smiled. "I'm glad I could help."

The lord rose. "I have disturbed your dinner again. You must forgive me. My manners are rusty. Very literally."

I chuckled then picked up my goblet of wine. "You are forgiven."

He bowed politely. "Good evening, Miss Hawking."

"And to you."

With that, the lord walked out of the hall. He rolled his sleeve back down as he went, rebuttoning it at the wrist. Before he exited, he looked over his shoulder at me, an odd expression on his metallic face.

"Miss Hawking? Do you like baked apples?" Mister Flint called as he returned from the kitchen.

Smiling, the lord exited the hall.

What an odd, odd mech. Grinning, I looked back at the automaton crossing the room toward me. The scent of freshly baked apples and cinnamon spiced the air. I picked up my fork and hoisted it like a saber. "I'm armed for the battle."

18
TEMPTING MORGAN LE FAY

I WOKE THE NEXT MORNING WITH RENEWED VIGOR. SETTING my books and Elyse's mirror aside, I grabbed what paper I could find from the writing desk and repacked my satchel. The sky overhead was a bit cloudy, but I wasn't going to let the rain stop me. Digging in the wardrobe once more, I discovered a light spring jacket that fit well but was worn by time. I slipped on the dark blue coat and headed toward the front of the castle.

To my surprise, the lord was waiting by the fireplace in the hall.

"Miss Hawking," he said, bowing to me. "I thought you might find this useful." He handed me a cylindrical leather package.

"What is it?" I asked.

"A map of the island."

"Oh! Oh, yes. This will be very helpful indeed. Thank you."

"The western side of the island only. I have your word?"

"Yes, of course. Best to avoid wolf country."

The lord chuckled, a sound that was surprisingly human. It was a shame I couldn't have a look at his voice box. The design of it amplified sound perfectly. When I returned to London, I would have much to consider regarding these mechanicals. Perhaps I could convince Missus Silver to tell me more about her creator.

"And to ensure your safety, I ask that you take a companion."

"Companion?"

He whistled. A moment later, I heard the quick sound of scurrying. The noise reminded me of street performers doing a tap dance. I was surprised when, a moment later, a dog appeared. Well, a dog but not a dog. The creature, like everything else on this island, was clockwork.

I knelt to look more closely at the beast. The dog had large golden optics and a metal tail that wagged happily. Its body was created from a color of bronze that was nearly red. Great care had been put into her creation.

"This is Kelly," he said. "She is a loyal companion."

"What manner of dog is she modeled after?"

"She's an Irish Setter."

"Hello, Kelly," I said, setting my hand on her head.

She wagged her tail happily.

"Well then, come along," I said, tapping my leg as I rose and headed toward the door. The cylinder for the map hung on a strap, which I strung around me.

"Western shore to the castle only," he reminded me.

"Of course," I said with a smile then headed outside.

ONCE I WAS out of the castle gates and in the forest once more, I felt the tension leave my body. It was beautiful in the forest. I had grown so accustomed to life in London that I never thought of the countryside.

Kelly snooped through the forest, nose to the ground, in the manner of a real dog. I eyed her skeptically. Who had created these fabulous creatures, and why had they been abandoned in this place?

I left the castle from the west gate and headed directly to the shoreline, only stopping once I reached the beach. I stared out at the dark blue waves which thundered against the shore. The smell of the sea filled my lungs. Kelly stood beside me staring out at the water. To my surprise, she whimpered.

Kneeling, my instinct was to pat her head, to comfort her. But why? She didn't actually feel anything, did she? The dog looked longingly at the water.

"You'll rust if you go play in the waves, won't you, poppet?"

The dog whimpered once more.

I was anthropomorphizing the mechanical. She was made to behave like a dog. Perhaps someone had designed her analytics to respond in such a manner when confronted with water to ensure she didn't get wet and rust out.

But still.

The large golden optics looked...sad.

"Shall we go look for the standing stones? Nothing to see here but pebbles anyway," I said to the dog then sat down on a piece of driftwood and pulled out the map. "We'll begin here and make a sweep. There seems to be some structure north of here. Noted here on the map," I told Kelly who seemed to be observing the map with me. I chuckled. "Clever girl. Can you read a map as well? There is a man in London I quite loathe, Gerard LeBoeuf, who is said to be the greatest cartographer in all of England. He advises all the explorers who go out on the seas to adventure. Detestable creature though. He says he loves me, but he tells that to every woman he meets. I wish I could find a gentleman who professes such passion but does so in earnest," I said with a laugh.

Taking one last glance at the map, I decided on my course. "Let's go find this mysterious structure, and we shall use it as our rallying point."

I gazed out at the sea one last time. Exploring the island was a distraction. More than anything, I hoped that Papa had made it to land safely and was busy arranging for a ship to come for me. But I couldn't think about that now. I didn't dare give into the thought that maybe Papa had not made it home.

"Come on, Kelly," I said then turned and headed back toward the interior of the island.

We walked under the thick limbs of the old oak trees deep into the lush green. Everything smelled fresh and alive. Keeping my eye on the landscape, the map in mind, I pushed through the dense woods until I spotted the ruins of a small structure ahead. Kelly ran toward it. From what I could tell, the place must been some sort of hermitage tucked into the forest away from the castle. Ivy and unusual orange-colored roses grew all around the Grecian-style columns. The small ruin was beautiful. Its gentle grace was a stark contrast to the metallic precision of the garden at the castle.

"What is this place?" I whispered to Kelly as I wove through the columns. The small ruin seemed to have been built to complement the natural surroundings. I was surprised to see some hints that it had frequently been used in the past, including a clock worked into the columns, the time on the face arrested close to nine o'clock. I passed through one section then found myself standing on a small veranda that overlooked a beautiful, picturesque scene. A brook meandered through the woods, emptying into a small pool on the rise just below the terrace. Somewhere in the trees above, a bird warbled happily. This place had been created to view the natural splendor. I imagined a painter or poet working from this very spot, calling up lines or dabbing green paint on a canvas.

Feeling content, I sat down on the flagstones and pulled out the map. Taking a pencil from my bag, I divided the landscape around me into four quarters, mindful to keep to the west of the island only. Wolves, right? I gazed back in the direction of the castle and east. Why was I supposed to avoid the mine? What had Missus Silver so upset?

I looked down at the map. The more hilly area of the island was all to the east and south of the castle. What had they been mining there? Had the mine run out? Why had all the equipment been left behind?

Frowning, I folded up my map. It didn't matter. Papa would return within the week. I'd make my study of the standing stones and the Ogham and see what I could learn about the automatons. I would keep busy until I could leave the island. The small hermitage would be my home base from which to explore. I rested a while longer then headed into the woods.

Kelly and I tromped through the ferns until we found the first of the standing stones. The menhir was covered in knot-work and Celtic designs. Sitting on the ground before the monolith, I sketched the rocks, copying each shape exactly. I also noted the Ogham writing on the stones. Digging in my bag for the writing paper and a piece of coal, I did a rubbing of the ancient language. Noting the stone on my map, I explored the rest of the woods only to find another small rock with a face like the one I'd seen when I'd first arrived and the other not far from the mine. This face wore a deep grimace. I noted it on the map and sketched it in my journal. I was almost done when Kelly, who'd been sniffing—or so she was tinkered to behave—through the ferns stiffened. Like a trained hunting dog, she lifted her leg in point, her back stiffening, tail straightening.

Rising, I followed her gaze.

She was staring into the forest on the eastern part of the

island where the trees were the thickest. A late-afternoon fog was rolling in from the sea, and the sky had grown cloudy as the day had progressed.

In the dark forest, I heard the sound of a tinkling bell and a soft laugh. I stared into the woods. Then I saw a shimmering blob of golden light.

Kelly growled.

I watched the strange glow as it bounced playfully then disappeared into the forest.

A wisp.

I looked down at the small stone with the face. My eyes deceived me for a moment when it appeared the face thereon was looking up at me.

"Well, Merlin. What tricks are you playing?" I called into the woods.

There was only silence and the strange feeling of eyes upon me.

"Or is it Morgan le Fay who haunts these woods?" I added.

To my surprise, I heard a soft laugh.

My skin prickled to goosebumps, and the hairs on the back of neck rose. If this was a holy island, a sacred place for Druids, it did not pay to play with things I didn't understand. Yet everything within me urged me to follow. To see where the wisp had gone. To know what was in that mine. No. Not a mine. To see what was in that cave.

I stepped toward the woods.

Kelly whimpered then trotted forward, blocking my path.

"The lord sent you to keep an eye on me, did he?"

The dog wagged her tail.

I stared into the forest. "I am too curious for my own good. It's true. Also, it may rain, and I won't have you getting wet. You win, Kelly. Let's head back to your castle."

The dog wagged her tail again. She turned and headed

back toward the castle, only pausing to look back expectantly at me.

"Coming," I said. I looked back at the forest one last time.

From the thick foliage, I could have sworn I heard a soft whisper.

Isabelle. Come.

19
WINDUP

KELLY AND I HAD JUST ENTERED THE CASTLE FOYER WHEN IT started to rain. Kelly disappeared somewhere deeper within the castle while I shrugged off my coat. I listened for the sounds of Missus Silver or Mister Flint or any of the other servants—or the lord—but heard nothing.

I eyed the castle steps. Perhaps this was my chance to learn more about the automatons.

Moving quickly and quietly, I worked my way up the stairs of the castle back to the turret hangar where I had found Papa. The place was empty. I closed the door behind me then set down my bag. I went to the workbench and began looking over all the tools. This workshop was that of an airship engineer, a mechanic. This was not the workshop of a clockwork tinker. That made no sense. In a house full of automatons, where were all the pieces and parts? Where were all the schematics? Where were the tools needed for fine work? I found nothing save sketches, equipment, and mechanics meant for airships. Old airships.

There were no answers here.

Frowning, I picked up a handful of blank paper and shoved

it in my bag. Tiptoeing, I slipped back out of the hangar and down the stairs once more.

"Ah, Miss Hawking. I was looking for you. Some tea, miss?" Mister Flint called, climbing the stairs toward me.

"Um. Yes. Please."

"Very good. I shall prepare high tea in the dining room," he said then turned around and headed back downstairs. I paused a few moments, pretending to look out the window until I was sure he had gone.

Then, creeping, I headed downstairs. All of my movements thus far had been restricted to the west wing of the castle. But there was a narrow hall on the first floor that led to the east wing. From what I could tell, the lord kept that wing to himself. Every time he appeared, that's where he'd come from. And that's where Kelly had run off to.

I turned and headed down the hallway. The wide hall had windows that looked out on the grounds on one side. On the other were rows of doors and even more corridors. I kept one ear listening for the lord or the servants then went exploring. The first hall was lined with oil paintings. Welsh lords and ladies, clearly aristocrats, were commemorated in their royal best, frozen in elegant poses. The paintings dated back many generations. When I reached the end of the hall, I noted a discolored spot on the wall where a canvas was missing. At the end of this hall, I found a staircase that led upward, presumably to the suites above and the other castle turret.

I had just made up my mind to risk his bad humor when I heard footsteps descending the stairs. I made out the distinct footfall of the lord followed by the padding of Kelly.

Frowning, I turned to the nearest door. Locked. I tried the next. Locked again.

The footsteps drew near.

I stuck my hand into my satchel and pulled out my small tool kit. Turning to the nearest door, I worked fast. A moment later, the lock popped. Opening the door gently, I slipped inside. I closed the door with a silent click just as the lord and his dog descended the stairs.

I listened, my heart pounding in my chest, as the lord and the dog passed.

Turning, I looked back into the room. There, on a long table at which at least twenty people could sit, was an endless mountain of windup keys.

Confused, I approached the table. The keys had been separated into piles: steel, copper, bronze, silver, gold, stone, and even some that looked to be made of glass. There were thousands of keys. Thousands. Each of the keys had a small tag. I lifted one of the steel keys. It was numbered: 8,015. I gazed around the room. There were chests sitting everywhere. Moving quietly, I opened a pinewood chest only to find more windup keys, all of which had been tagged.

A slow realization washed over me.

The lord was searching for his key. That made no sense. Couldn't someone just tinker a mold for him? And where had all these keys come from?

I froze when I heard voices drift down the hallway. It was Missus Silver and the lord. I scanned all around the room looking for a place to hide, a place to escape. There was none. But I also noticed that sitting in one corner was a large painting covered with a drape. The portrait from the hall? Why was it here?

Dismissing the idea for the moment, I hurried across the room, opened the window, and slipped outside. It was a tight fit getting around the iron topiary positioned there, but I took a deep breath and slid past the metallic ornament as I closed the window behind me. Once clear, I ducked low.

"And in today's chest?" Missus Silver asked.

"Nothing," the lord replied flatly. "You know the game. Of course, there was nothing."

"The girl—Miss Hawking—surely she could help you. She is a very gifted tinker. Perhaps if you let her examine you, she might find a way—"

"No."

"But, my lord, she is a very bright and honest girl. Perhaps if we just tell her what has happened to us, she will believe us. She will help us."

"Say nothing. This is my burden to bear. I must be the one to undo the curse."

"If you won't tell her, then, at least... I am not sure how to put it, my lord, but she is the first woman to come to this island since...since it happened. Don't you think she might be the one to help break the curse?"

"I will not trouble that poor girl. You're right. She is honest and bright, and she is also gorgeous. She doesn't deserve to be drowned by our misery. Her father will return, and she will go. And soon, my heart will stop, and that will be the end of it. When I am gone, you will be restored."

"But, my lord, you could at least try. If not for us, at least for yourself. She is an amiable creature, really."

"Amiable, yes, but also very unusual."

"Time has passed. The manners of the day have no doubt changed."

"I am sure you are right. No, there is no fault in her. The fault is in me. Look at me, Aelwyd. What is there for any woman to consider?"

"My lord...Rhys...what's in a face? It is the heart that matters most."

The lord laughed in a deep, tinny voice that rattled. "And what heart have I shown her? Have you seen her arm? *I* did that. *Me.* I can barely look her in the face," he said then paused. "Do you feel the breeze? The window latch is open."

Gasping, I turned and quickly darted away from the open window. My heart pounding in my chest, I raced around the front of the castle toward the gate and out of sight. Surely he had not seen me.

I dashed to the front door and stood for a moment under the eave away from the rain.

A curse.

The place was cursed.

Well, no wonder it had been abandoned.

But cursed by whom? What had the lord meant? I replayed the conversation in my head, but it didn't sound like anything to me. I couldn't make sense of it. The thought that he found me admirable, if odd, made my heart beat quicker. Why? He was just an automaton. What did his opinion matter? But all the same, the compliment affected me. But their words...the curse...what did it all mean?

Moving fast, I slipped inside once more then headed toward the dining room. I arrived just in time to find Mister Flint setting out the tea.

"Ah, Miss Hawking. Good timing. Please," he said, pulling out a chair.

My heart still racing, I slid into my seat, relieved that the room was dim enough that he didn't notice that I was damp from the rain.

"Not the freshest tea, I must confess. And I do apologize. It may be a bit more herb than Earl Grey."

"It's all right. I have work to focus on anyway. Hardly ever even notice my plate in such a state, I confess," I said as I began unpacking my satchel. "But I'll begin in good form," I said, picking up a bite of the apple from the plate and popping it into my mouth.

Mister Flint laughed. "Good appetite, yes. Your form, however...you know I did set you out some flatware."

I felt my cheeks redden. No, you would never catch a refined lady eating with her fingers. I grinned. "What? And give you something else to wash. I didn't want you to get rusty from the exertion."

"I'm so pleased you thought of me, mistress."

"But of course."

The mech laughed again, bowed, then headed back to the kitchen.

I rose, spreading my papers all around. The sunlight in the dining room, despite its broad windows, was abysmal. The heavy velvet drapes blocked what sun came in during the afternoon. Frowning, I took a sip of the tea.

He was right. I tasted rosemary, mint, and lavender, but not much tea, per se. All in all, it still tasted fine.

Then I got to work.

Opening my journal, I looked at the sketches of the stones and tried to make connections. What similar symbols had I seen? And what commonalities had there been in the Ogham?

But my mind went back to the conversation I'd overheard. What had Missus Silver been talking about? What had happened to them? And why was it the lord's cross to the bear?

The lord.

No. Missus Silver—Aelwyd—had called him something else.

She had called him Rhys.

20
THE LIBRARY

I DON'T KNOW HOW LONG I SPENT SORTING THROUGH MY notes, but when I took another sip of my tea it was cold. It was dreadfully dim in the dining room. Frowning, I lifted the papers, trying to see them in the last of the dying sunlight.

When I looked up, I realized the lord was standing there.

When had he arrived?

"I'm sorry. I didn't hear you come in."

"So I noticed," he said then motioned to my work. "You're cataloging the symbols on the stones?"

"Yes. And the Ogham," I said then shook my head. "But the light in here has finished the job for the day."

The lord nodded thoughtfully. "Collect your things. I have somewhere better for you to work."

Curious, I tidied up my papers and journal and stuffed them back into my bag which he politely took from my hands.

"Come," he said, motioning to me.

Grabbing the map, I followed him.

He led me from the dining room toward a section of the house I had not yet explored. As we walked, I noticed the beautiful oil paintings on the walls. These were not portraits.

Instead, they were artistic renderings of fruits, flowers, animals, and even woodland scenes.

"These are divine," I said, stopping to eye a painting of a bright red rose. The artist's use of color and the perceived movement of the strokes reminded me of Van Gogh.

"The lady of this house was a gifted artist," the lord said as he studied the painting as well. He sighed heavily then asked, "Is the paint still very red?"

"Red? Yes. Alive as can be," I said then turned to him. "Your optics don't detect color?"

"Not anymore. This was always my favorite painting. The red was arresting. Now all I see is black, white, and gray. My vision has become much like my mind."

"I could have a look at your optics. Perhaps you have a short?"

The lord laughed. "That is very kind of you, Miss Hawking, but, it's no use," he said then turned and continued down the hallway.

I stopped once more when I spotted a painting of a dog on the wall. The artist was different. This hand had less artistic flow and more realistic symmetry. The dog in the painting had large, amber-colored eyes. "This looks like Kelly," I said.

The lord paused. His hands behind his back, he considered the painting. "The work of an amateur. But, yes, it does resemble an Irish Setter."

"Not an amateur. The style is different from the other artist, but no less creative. The realism is perfect. Look, you can even see a shadow of the artist in the dog's eyes. No. This is the hand of an observer. And an astute one," I leaned in and studied the painting. I could see that the figure reflected in the dog's eyes was male, but not more than that.

I looked up at the lord who was smiling.

"What?" I asked.

He shook his head. "Nothing. Perhaps you are right, Miss

Hawking. This way," he said. He led us down several more corridors then, at the end of the hall, pushed open a set of wide double doors.

"I think you will find the light much better in here."

I stepped into the massive room behind him.

Unable to suppress a gasp, I stared in wonder. Reaching two stories in height, I stood at the entrance to a massive library. The u-shaped room had floor-to-ceiling windows. At the top of each window were mosaics in colored glass which sent shimmering rainbows of light on the floor. Between each window, on both the first and second floor, was a bookshelf. Winding stairs on both sides of the entrance led to a balcony on the second floors. Bookshelves reached from the floor to the ceiling. The top shelves were only accessible by the ladders on the balcony. At the opposite end of the room was a massive fireplace. A portrait of a man, woman, and child—all dressed in regal fashion—hung over the fireplace. A long table ran down the center of the room. The sweet scent of old books filled the air.

"Missus Silver mentioned you had some books with you and that one had been ruined in the shipwreck. I asked her to learn the titles of your books. Please forgive the intrusion. She said there was a volume on Hero of Alexandria." The lord went to the table and set his hand on a stack of five volumes in blue leather. "These books are on the Greek inventors, including Hero of Alexandria. And this is a tome by Mister Graves on Celtic knotwork. He mentions Ogham in passing. It's not much, but a start. Please feel free to use the library as you wish. Were you planning to go out into the forest again tomorrow?"

"I... Thank you. Yes."

He nodded. "I will accompany you," he said. He set my satchel and papers on the table then picked up another book that had been there and tucked it under his arm. "Do you need anything else?"

I shook my head. "No. I hardly know what to say. It's so lovely," I said, looking around once more. My head was spinning. And I had thought Mister Denick's shop, the little Library of Alexandria at Hungerford, was a sight to behold. This place was a million times grander.

He smiled. "I'm glad it pleases you. The library is yours," he said then turned and headed back down the hall.

Gratitude swelling in my chest, I gazed after him. He had such a regal walk and stance, and despite being made of cogs and gears, there was a kindness to him that I couldn't put my finger on.

Odd.

Swallowing an excited squeal, I set the map down and lifted the small book on Celtic knots, opening the book and inhaling deeply. Perfection.

Maybe being lost on this strange little island wasn't so bad after all.

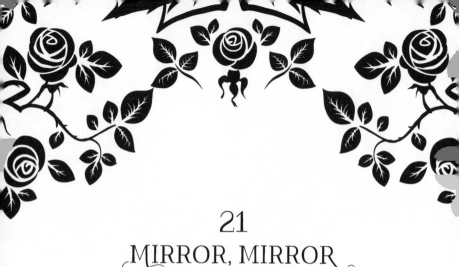

21
MIRROR, MIRROR

MISTER FLINT BROUGHT MY DINNER TO THE LIBRARY WHERE I sat working later into the night. The gas lamps overhead and on the walls bathed the room in light. The grandfather clock in the hallway had just struck midnight when I felt a hand on my shoulder.

"Miss Hawking," Missus Silver said. "Why don't you get some rest? I'll leave your work here just as you have it."

Yawning tiredly, I rose.

"Yes, you're right. The fire is burning down anyway," I said, casting a glance toward the fireplace. My eyes went once more to the portrait above. "Missus Silver, who are they?" I asked.

"Oh, that's our late lord and lady and their son," she said, sounding suddenly overly dismissive.

I eyed the painting carefully. The fashions depicted in the picture, much like everything else in the castle, were dated. But there was something more. The lord in the painting...his face looked somewhat familiar. The lord stood with his hands behind his back. The lady stood with her hand on her son's shoulder. The small boy had bright gray eyes, curly black hair, and a bright smile.

"So you were under the lord's employ?"

"Yes, until he passed. And then his son."

"And the lady?"

"Passed away not long after the portrait was made."

"And the young lord?"

A strange click emitted from Missus Silver. "I almost forgot. I brought you a shawl, Miss Hawking. It's very cool in the hall-way," Missus Silver said, setting a warm wrap around my shoulders. "Now, why don't you head up to bed? I've laid everything out for you. I'll be by in the morning to see if you need anything."

"The young lord," I said, turning back to the portrait once more. "Is he still alive? If not him, his family? Does the family know you all are here on your own? Perhaps someone in the family should be informed of your condition. When I return to London, I can write to the estate and inquire."

"Never mind that, Miss Hawking. Our master knows where we are and looks out for us as best he can. Now, off to bed with you."

I looked at the smirking smile of the child once more. The boy was full of mirth. I could see it behind his eyes, but still, he sought to temper his smile. When I looked up at the elder lord in the painting, I could see why. From his hawkish expression to his firm stance, everything about the elder master showed him to be a hard man. The lady, however, had a free and open face. The mirth in the boy's eyes was reflected in his mother's. Sighing, I thought once more about the conversation I had overheard earlier that day. There was undoubtedly trouble here if the mechs thought they were cursed. Perhaps their circuitry was not capable of handling what appeared to be their total abandonment. Despite her assurances, I needed to help them.

The lord—Rhys—took care of the others, but still. I must be able to do something for them.

Sighing, I pulled the shawl around me, grabbed my journal and a candle, then smiled at Missus Silver. "Goodnight."

"Goodnight, dear," she said then turned and went to the fireplace.

I headed back down the hallway. It was chilly in the castle and very silent. I paused when I got to the main foyer. There was noise coming from the hallway that led to the east wing. Tiptoeing, I went to investigate.

Light poured from around the door to the room where I'd found the windup keys. From inside, I heard someone shifting metal. Someone was digging through the keys. I debated. It was the lord, I was sure, and I knew what he was searching for. I could help him. I could easily make a mold of his key, but that would require his permission. Something told me that although he was warming up to me a bit, it didn't pay to push.

Turning, I headed back upstairs to my chamber.

I set my candle and journal down on the writing desk and changed into my dressing robes. Someone had kept the fire stoked, and the room was warm. I went to the writing desk. A clockwork rose like the one my father had taken, which had earned the mechanical lord's ire was sitting in a vase on the desk. I lifted the rose. I would need to spend some time studying the mechanics inside. Perhaps tomorrow, after my study of the forest, I could open the bloom and inspect its mechanics. Of course, I would need the lord's permission. He was so particular about everything. I shook my head. I was trapped in this place until my father returned, but what a place in which to be held captive. From the standing stones to the mechanicals to the library, everywhere I looked, I found something that excited my curiosity beyond measure. I blew out the flame on my candle but was puzzled when a bright light shone into my eyes.

A corner of the wrapping on Elyse's magic mirror—I still chuckled thinking of that one—had slipped aside. The mirror was reflecting the bright moonlight pouring in through the window. I unwrapped the mirror and looked within. I was a terrible mess. My hair had fallen into a messy bun. Apparently, at some point, I had stuffed a pencil behind my ear for safe-keeping. And there was a leaf in my hair. Had that been there since I'd been outside earlier today?

"What man could ever love a fright like me?" I said with a laugh.

The moonlight in the mirror glowed bright, and for a moment, the silver handle shimmered blue. To my astonishment, my reflection faded from the looking glass as the image turned smoky. Wide-eyed, I stared as the image sharpened once more.

I saw the ruins of the little hermitage in the forest. As the image cleared, I saw a man standing on the veranda overlooking the beautiful pool of water. He was poised before an easel, painting the beautiful scene.

Lifting my hand tepidly, I reached out to touch the looking glass.

The man in the image stopped and turned, looking out of the glass at me.

I gasped.

Hands shaking, I quickly set the mirror back on the table, covering it once more with the scarf.

It...it couldn't be. My heart pounded in my chest. It couldn't be. The man in the mirror had been the mechanical lord himself, but in the flesh. A real, living man. And he had smiled sweetly at me, his eyes full of love.

HANDS TREMBLING, my breath quick, I went to the window and set my forehead on the cool window pane.

I was tired. That was all. I had worked too much, was too distraught. And I had hit my head in the shipwreck. I'd been practically unconscious for days. I had over-exerted myself today. I was just seeing things.

Yes. I was seeing things.

I was seeing the lord, the mechanical, as a living man. A young, handsome lord with dark hair and silver-colored eyes. A young lord dressed in an antiquated fashion.

Leaning back, I shook my head. It made no sense. First, how could the mirror even show such an image. And then, how or why would it show me that?

Perhaps…perhaps the true lord of this castle had created the automaton in the family image. Was there a real lord somewhere, a man of flesh and blood, who looked like his machine? Was I meant to find the real lord of this castle and return him to this place? Yes, that had to be it. Somewhere a living man existed. His creator had fashioned him in the family image, that was all. I needed to find him.

And say what?

How do you do, Lord Somebody. So, I discovered a forgotten island that appears to belong to your ancestors. Lost the map there, did you? Well, the mechs there have taken charge of the castle, one of them calling himself the lord of the place. I'm sure he's just trying to keep everything in order. He seems very nice, really. Comes off a bit beastly at first, but quite a gentleman if you give him a chance. Anyway, they do seem like a good lot, but they are in need of repair and your castle is falling apart. Shall I take you there? Oh, and I do love the place beyond all measure. Since you appeared to me in a magic mirror, I think we are supposed to be together. Why don't you go ahead and marry me and make me Lady Whatever and move me to your little island where we can live happily ever after?

Right? So. No. I exhaled deeply. Elyse's fairy tales, exhaustion, and my concussion were working an enchantment on me. I needed to sleep.

I slipped into the bed and tried not to think about the lord in the mirror. I tried not to think about the twisting feeling I'd gotten in my stomach when he had smiled. I tried not to think about how everything inside of me wanted that unknown man, unknown person, without reason.

And I desperately tried not to think about the fact that the living lord looked exactly like the mechanical lord downstairs.

No. I would definitely not think about that.

But when I closed my eyes, I imagined that young lord putting his hand in mine, and it was everything I had ever dreamed of.

22
MATILDA

I WOKE THE NEXT MORNING FEELING FOOLISH. I'D BEEN HALF asleep when I'd returned to my chamber the night before. I'd let visions and superstition get the better of me. Thinking of it no more, I redressed in my walking clothes and headed back downstairs. Stopping first at the library, I collected some of my papers and notes and packed them into my satchel. I eyed the painting over the fireplace once more. Fairy stories. I'd have to amuse Elyse with tales of the effect her magic mirror had on my wits when I got back to London. Readying myself, I headed to the main castle foyer.

The lord and Kelly were waiting, the lord dressed for an outing. It seemed odd to see a gentleman wearing a wide-brimmed Cavalier hat in the style favored by King Charles. Well, man was a matter of speaking. This was an automaton. And trapped on this island, he would have no sense of fashions of the time.

"I packed you a breakfast, Miss Hawking," Missus Silver said.

"I hope you don't mind. I thought it was such a lovely

morning that maybe you'd enjoy breakfast outside," the lord said.

"Thank you," I said.

Taking the basket from Missus Silver, he signaled to Kelly, and we headed outside.

"Yesterday you had a look at the northern quadrant?" he asked.

"Yes. I thought I'd begin at the hermitage and go northwest today."

He nodded thoughtfully. "You will find stones there. I can show you."

I smiled up at him, surprised and puzzled to see him looking down at me, a smirking smile on his mechanical face.

My stomach knotted. Surely the tinker who'd made him had modeled him after the family. I forced my attention away from the lord and back to the forest. Papa would return soon, and I wouldn't have to trouble myself with any of this anymore. Very soon, an airship would appear over the castle, and it would all be over.

We headed out, passing the perfect garden arrested in metal then back into the forest. It was quiet amongst the trees. The weather was warm and sunny. We walked along together in quiet contemplation. The silence felt comfortable.

Kelly ran ahead as we neared the hermitage.

From inside the lord's body, I heard a series of clicks.

He coughed uncomfortably as if to hide the noise. "Here we are," he said. "She still stands."

"You don't come out here?"

"No. Not in many years."

We stepped into the opened structure, really more a gazebo than a home, and walked to the veranda overlooking the pond. The lord stopped and gently touched one of the roses growing on the column. I watched as his optics focused repeatedly.

"It's orange," I said. "Like the sunset. A mix of orange, yellow, and pink. The colors bleed into one another."

He smiled. "Thank you, Miss Hawking."

"Isabelle."

"Pardon?"

"Isabelle. That's my name. You may call me Isabelle if you like."

"Isabelle," he repeated. "I'm more commonly known as Rhys."

I smiled. "Nice to meet you, Rhys," I said playfully, extending my hand.

The mech took my hand into his, bowed, then laid a metallic kiss on my gloved fingers. "The pleasure is mine," he said then let me go.

The gesture so surprised me that I felt a blush brighten my cheeks. How ridiculous. He was an automaton. Metal, and cogs, and bolts, and wires...

"Here," Rhys said, picking the prettiest bloom on the vine. It was a simple rosebud, just barely opened. Ensuring there were no thorns, the mechanical gently set the flower in my hair above my ear. I was pleased to see his grip was working well enough to do such delicate work.

I chuckled, touching the blossom. "Thank you, kind sir."

"Of course," he said with a smile. He selected another rose, adding it to his lapel, then looked out at the view. Once more, a series of clicks emanated from his chest. He was still for so long I almost wondered if something within him had broken.

"Rhys?" I said, gently setting my hand on his arm.

He jerked oddly as if reanimating himself. Had he had been lost in thought? "Yes. Very well. Let's explore, shall we? This way...Isabelle."

The automaton turned and headed away from the hermitage into the forest.

We headed into the thick woods. It was so beautiful that I

pitied the mechanical that he couldn't see the vibrant palette of greens and smell the loam of the earth. It was enchanting beyond compare.

Rhys led me to the first ring, a small place with five tall stones and a center altar. The feel of magic filled the air so strongly that my skin rose in goosebumps.

"This place…everywhere I go, I feel magic."

Rhys stared at the stones. "Even at the castle?"

I frowned. "There is a different kind of magic to be had there. But no, not there."

He nodded. "No. Not there." Reaching out to touch the stone, he hesitated then drew his hand back. "The lady of the castle, the one who made the rose painting, could feel the magic here as well. She used to run barefoot in the forest. She said she could feel the magic coursing between her toes."

I smiled. "The lady…is she the same woman in the painting that hangs in the library?"

Again, something inside of Rhys clicked. "Yes."

"She was lovely."

"Yes. In mind, body, and spirit. A fey thing, some called her."

I eyed the mech. I wanted to unload a million questions upon him, but even one at a time felt like I was pushing. But still, the vision in the mirror haunted me. It felt like answers hung just beyond my grasp, and my intellect could barely stand it. "The lady in the painting seemed quite in contrast with the gentleman in the portrait."

The mech huffed a laugh. "A more different pair never existed."

"Some say there is synergy in opposites."

"Not in those opposites," he said, his voice turning cold. "Now, here are some of the Ogham symbols you are hunting."

I went to the stone and looked at the writing engraved

thereon, cognizant of the fact that Rhys had changed the subject. "That's odd," I said, pulling out my journal.

"Odd?"

"The Ogham writing. It's the same as on the other ring of stones. See," I said, pointing from my journal to the stone. "The figures are the same. I hadn't noticed before."

"What does it say?"

"I'm...I'm not sure. I'll need to work on it," I said, again writing down the combination of slashes along a single line that made up the Ogham. I went from stone to stone, sketching both the stones and the Celtic figures and knotwork thereon in my book.

Kelly raced through the forest chasing everything she could see, including waving blades of grass. The lord circled the stones as well, eyeing the ancient structures with interest, but his arms stayed folded behind his back. From time to time, he would look over my shoulder at my sketches.

"Your technique is very good, albeit mechanical."

"Mechanical?"

"Precise, perhaps, is the better word. It is the hand of an engineer. Your skill for catching the real form is superb."

I flipped back to earlier pages in my journal. While some had blurred due to getting wet, others had survived. I turned to my sculpture of the birds that sang Vivaldi.

"This was one of my best pieces. I worked all winter on it. The birds moved in tune to Vivaldi's *Allegro-Largo-Allegro.*"

"Ah yes, Vivaldi. That new piece is quite in fashion. I've only heard it once."

"New piece?" Vivaldi's work was almost a hundred years old.

Rhys turned and looked at me, studying me carefully. From within him, I heard a series of odd clicks. "Well, I mean, it's well-marked, that's all. Your sculpture. What happened to it?"

"Papa and I were on our way to Islay for a wedding. The piece was intended as a wedding gift. It's somewhere at the bottom of the sea now," I said, turning the pages so the lord could see the interior designs of the sculpture. "As you can see, the sculpture was a marriage of clockwork, music, and movement."

"My servants and I must prove interesting subjects for you," he said. His voice held a tone of resentment I didn't understand. Why would he be angry for me being in interested in his design?

I eyed him carefully, once more seeing the lines of the face in the painting in the library.

"There is beauty in all forms. Steel, flesh, or stone," I said, setting my hand on the standing stone once more. "All have their beauties."

The lord harrumphed, making me wonder if he had some sort of inflatable in his chest that mimicked the lungs—a creation in which my father would be very interested—then turned and moved on to the next monolith.

When I was done sketching the stones, we headed deeper into the woods. Rhys surprised me, gently holding my arm and guiding me over small streams. Had he been programmed to act the part of the perfect gentleman?

The next stone we found was one of unique design. On a rise that looked toward the ocean was a round stone with a hole at its center. In the distance was another rock, this one cone-shaped. I pulled out my map.

"Here," he said, noting a position on the map. He stared off at the horizon.

I noted the location of the stones on the map then leaned down to look through the hole. "Makes you wonder what it's pointing at."

"The Isle of Man."

"Are you certain?"

He nodded. "And on Anglesey, you will find a similar set of stones pointing here."

I looked through the hole. "What do you suppose will happen if I pass through?" I said, moving as if to enter.

The lord reached down and gently held my arm. "Isabelle. Do not."

I was startled by the sound of panic in his voice. I looked up at him. "Rhys?"

He chuckled lightly. "Just…best not to tempt fate. That was what my mother—er, my master, always told me. Especially in this place."

I stared at him. *Mother?* I narrowed my eyes as I considered. "Very well. This seems a good a place as any to have a quick bite to eat. Do you mind? I don't want to waste your time, but," I said, setting my hand on my stomach.

"No. Not at all." He handed the basket to me. "I think there was some claret in there."

"No oil for you?"

He laughed lightly. "No."

Inside, I found a small hunk of dense bread, salted fish, and wine. Everything the servants were cooking were things they had scavenged from the island—save the wine.

I poured myself a small glass and sipped as I stared out at the waves.

"Do you remember the shipwreck?" Rhys asked.

"No. And for that, I am grateful. I was asleep when the weather turned. I fell from my bunk. Papa and I went on deck only to see the tempest. I was swept over. I remember hitting my head, then nothing until I woke up on this beach. But I think I remember snow."

"Snow?"

"During the tempest. I'd swear that it was snowing. A rare summer squall? Perhaps some fluke in the weather? I don't know. I remember it being white and cold, then the darkness and the waves."

"That is very strange," he said, staring back toward the forest.

"Indeed."

I ate my breakfast—though it was now after lunch—then packed up the basket once more.

"Speaking of the weather," he said, motioning to the sky. As the day had progressed, the sky had grown gray and cloudy. "As far as I know, there are no other stones in this section of your map. Perhaps we should head back?"

I nodded. "I don't want you and Kelly caught out here in the rain."

"Thank you," he said then whistled for his dog who appeared a few moments later, a parcel in her mouth.

I chuckled at the sight of her. "I was worried the selkies found you."

"What do you have there?" Rhys called.

Wagging her tail, Kelly set a very wet package at his feet. The parcel, despite the paper covering being ripped, the pack waterlogged, looked familiar.

"Wait," I said, kneeling. "There was debris from the ship-wreck on this beach. That package…" I said then pushed off the wet paper. Digging in my satchel, I pulled out a knife and cut the twine holding the light wooden box closed.

"What is it?" Rhys asked.

"This package is mine."

"Yours?"

"It must have washed ashore." I carefully removed the lid of the box to find a soaking wet ball gown inside. It was the yellow dress I'd packed to wear to the wedding. "Impossible. Dear Kelly, how did you ever find this of all things? What chance!"

The dog wagged her mechanical tail happily.

Rhys made a strange sound, a sort of frustrated grunt, then glared into the woods. "Very improbable."

From the forest beyond us, I swore I heard a tinkling laugh.

I closed the lid on the box. "It will need to be washed and hung to dry. It was a very expensive gown. High fashion, Papa called it," I said with a chuckle. "I'm glad it survived," I said, staring down the beach. Maybe I should come back and have another look through the wreckage. Perhaps other gems had washed ashore. But given the darkening sky, now was not the time. "Good girl," I said, patting Kelly on the head.

"I'm pleased for you," he said, reaching out to carry the package for me.

"Please. Allow me. It's quite wet," I cautioned.

He pulled his hand back. "Yes, you're right." Offering me his arm, we turned and headed back into the woods. As we walked, I heard the same songbird that I'd noticed before, its sound so sweet and strange.

Rhys stilled and looked into the trees. "Do you hear that?" he asked.

I nodded. "I heard it the last time I was out. Such a pretty songbird."

To my surprise, he repeated the bird's call. The soft, sweet song emanated from somewhere deep within him.

There was a pause, and the bird whistled in reply.

The lord repeated the call.

I watched the trees only to see a glimmer of gold and movement amongst the leaves.

The pair exchanged calls again.

Then, on the wide oak above me, the bird alighted on a branch. The tiny winged creature was gold-colored. But that was because it appeared to be literally made of gold and every bit as clockwork as the lord himself.

The little bird warbled once more then hopped down the branch to move closer to Rhys.

The lord held out his arm, extending a finger. The bird turned his head, eyeing him skeptically.

"Come, Matilda," he called gently.

I stood perfectly still as I watched the exchange.

The bird chirped sweetly then flitted down and landed on Rhys's finger.

I was shocked.

Moving gently, Rhys gently stroked the metal feathers on the clockwork bird's head.

But from somewhere deep within the forest, that same strange wind blew once more. The little clockwork bird chirped nervously then turned and looked into the forest. The sound of a tinkling bell and a light laugh was carried on the wind. The tiny bird chirped loudly then turned and flew away.

The lord stepped away from me and turned to face the dark glen, staring down the strange wind, an angry look on his face.

Overhead, the sky rumbled, and lightning streaked the horizon.

Again, I heard a laugh, but this time, I heard menace.

"Rhys?"

He didn't answer.

I stared into the dark forest. There was something there. I could feel it, but I didn't know what.

"Rhys?" I said softly, reaching out to him. "Come on. Let's get you and Kelly inside before it rains."

He stood another moment more looking out at the darkening woods.

"Yes. Very well," he said then turned and joined me, linking his arm in mine. The act seemed almost subconscious if such a thing was possible.

Frowning, I stared in the direction of the dark woods.

What was on the eastern side of the island? What force was there that so disturbed everyone in the castle? Again, I was reminded of Missus Silver's words. A curse. The castle was cursed. Was that true? Was such a thing even possible? But by what? Whom? And why?

We walked in silence back toward the castle as the dark clouds overhead gathered once more. The lord pushed open the gate for Kelly and me, and we entered the metal garden. Retaking my arm, we walked toward the castle.

"So, Matilda?"

"She used to live in the castle. She was a pet. She escaped by chance. I'm glad to see she survived. I have worried about her out there exposed to the elements."

"Pretty songbird. Such a rare sound."

"She was a gift. Someone brought her from Barbados many years ago."

I looked back toward the woods. The ancient trees waved menacingly as the sky grew dark. I suddenly felt very, very sad for the mechanicals. Forgotten or cursed—I didn't know which —their plight was pitiable.

But which was it: forgotten or cursed?

I gazed off to the east. There was something in the woods. Whatever it was, it held the key. I knew where to go to learn my answer. Now I just had to muster enough courage to seek it out.

23
CLANDESTINE AFFAIRS

AFTER WE RETURNED, RHYS RETREATED TO HIS WING OF THE castle, and I headed back to the library. Sitting before my maps and notes, I found myself distracted. I gazed up at the painting above the fireplace, studying the expressions of the three people there. What had happened here? Where had all the people gone?

"Tea, mistress?" Mister Flint said, carrying in a tray. "And Missus Smith sent some sweets for you."

Once more, I noticed the limp with which he walked. As well, his optic didn't seem to sit quite right.

"Thank you," I said with a sigh, turning from the portrait. "Mister Flint, would you like me to have a look at your leg and optic? Perhaps there is something I can do."

Mister Flint paused as he considered. "The optic is as it should be. But if you would be willing to have a look at my knee, I would be much obliged."

He set down the tray while I grabbed the tools from inside my satchel.

I tried not to giggle when the mech pulled up his hose to reveal his metallic leg. It wasn't so much the movement or the hose that were amusing, but the modest expression on the man's face. How could a mechanical face express so much emotion?

Kneeling on the ground, I had a look at the wires. While the mechanism seemed to be intact, it appeared that a cog deep within the knee joint had rusted.

"We'll need to replace a part then give it a good lube," I said. "I might have something that will do the trick. But do you have any replacement parts? And some oil?"

"I…well, yes. Yes, Miss Hawking."

"Very good. And a workbench? It will be easier if you are lying down."

"Oh. Well, yes. Very well, come with me," he said then motioned for me to follow.

We headed back down the hallway to the east wing of the castle, passing the room with all the windup keys, to another door on the first floor. Casting a glance toward the steps that led to the upper floors, Mister Flint led me into another room.

"It's a rather shoddy workshop, but we've done the best we can," he said.

The room had once been some kind of study but was transformed. Tools lay on a table as well as parts that looked like they had once belonged to a clock, some torn up household tools, garden equipment, and a few other devices I could not recognize. Clearly, they'd scavenged for the parts they needed. There was a table at the center of the room.

"Here you are," Mister Flint said, motioning to the parts table. He picked up a small can of oil and handed it to me.

Grabbing what parts were there, I hoped I would be able to make at least a small improvement.

"Very well. If you don't mind lying down," I said, motioning to the table.

"Oh. Yes. All right," he said, sitting hopping up on the workbench.

His apprehension moved me. Suddenly I felt more like a doctor than a tinker.

I set my hand on his shoulder. "This may feel a bit... uncomfortable. Shall I turn you off until the repair is completed?"

The mech took a windup key from his pocket and handed it to me. He then removed his coat and unbuttoned and removed his shirt. Whoever had created him had instilled such a sense of modesty in him that I swore I felt him blushing. "On my back, as with Missus Silver, you will find my windup. Turn the key as far as you can without strain. Once you remove the key, I will reactivate. To turn me off, simply turn the key widdershins," he said.

I nodded. Taking the key in hand, I slipped it into the hole on his back. "I'll take good care of you. I promise," I said.

"Thank you," he replied, and then I turned the key counterclockwise, shutting down the mechanical.

The ticking inside him slowed, and his optics dimmed.

I lowered him slowly and carefully onto the table so I could have a better look at his leg. The piece that was giving him trouble was buried deep within the knee. I really needed my own tools. It was obvious the workshop had been thrown together by the automatons, who were decidedly not tinkers. At the moment, however, what I most needed was a magnifying glass. I set down my tools and began hunting around the room. There was nothing on the table, so I started looking through the shelves. Those, too, turned up empty. I went to the enormous closet. Most of the previous contents of the study had been moved there. I looked through dust-covered boxes until I finally found a box that contained a magnification glass. It had been housed with a number of frames that contained specimens of butterflies. I was about to close the closet once more when I spotted an odd draped shape in one corner. Moving carefully, I removed the draping off what I had expected to be a statue or a suit of armor only to find another automaton.

I gasped.

The mech was a maid dressed in a similar fashion to Missus Silver. But something about her appearance gave her a youthful look. Like Missus Silver, her face was made of porcelain.

I cast a glance at the door, then at Mister Flint. No harm in having a peek.

I looked the automaton over. Her panel in the back was open. She'd shorted out. I studied her wiring and cogs. From what I could see, it looked like she'd gotten wet.

I looked back at Mister Flint then at the maid. Tapping my finger on my chin as I thought, I left her for the moment and returned to work on Mister Flint. Holding the magnifying glass in one hand and my tools in the other, I was able to remove the rusted piece from Mister Flint's leg and replace it with another, newer—but not new—gear. I set the piece in place then oiled the joint. It took a few adjustments, but finally, his knee had better range of movement and no more squeak when I bent it.

I then set my tools aside and eyed the maid once more. It felt like a pity to just leave her there. The least I could do was try.

Leaving Mister Flint on the table, I returned to the closet. There, I found a wooden dolly. Grunting from the effort, I loaded the maid onto the dolly then wheeled her to the window so I could have a better look.

Under the sunlight—though dim since a light raining was falling—I got a better look. As I had guessed, she had shorted out. A ton of her wires had corroded. It looked like someone had attempted to repair or replace her parts but had failed. I went to the workbench and fingered through the supplies there. Not much on hand.

Then I remembered seeing a spool of wire in the hangar in the turret.

Debating, I left both mechs and hurried up the stairs to the airship hangar. From somewhere deep in the castle, I heard Missus Silver and Rhys talking. Wincing, I knew I needed to be fast.

I rushed up the steps to the turret, relieved to discover the door was unlocked. Moving quickly, I grabbed the spool of wire off the workbench. I then dug into the workbench drawers in search of a small screwdriver. I found plyers, bolts, and even an old compass, but no screwdriver. Digging in the very back of the last drawer, I unearthed a handful of paper, but alas, no screwdriver. I slipped the tools into my pocket, dropping the papers back into the drawer, but then I paused a moment. These were not just simple papers. They were letters addressed to Lord Rhys Llewellyn. On second thought, I slipped the letters into my pocket.

I grinned. First, I would sneakily repair the broken automaton. When I was done, I would snoop through the mail. I was becoming very good at clandestine activities. One day, I would make a good busybody.

Slipping out of the hangar, I headed downstairs. To my great relief, I spotted Missus Silver and Rhys through the window. While it was still raining, the pair was walking with an umbrella toward the east gate of the garden.

I raced back to the workshop. My heart pounding in my chest, I closed the door behind me.

Mister Flint still lay on the table. I felt great pity seeing him like that, but he'd have to wait just a bit longer.

I grabbed a stool and settled in behind the maid.

"Well, my dear. Let's see what I can do for you," I said, then leaned in and got to work.

24
REUNIONS

THERE WAS FAR MORE DAMAGE TO THE FEMALE AUTOMATON than I had initially thought. The rough tools in the workshop were below subpar—if there was such a thing—but after some work and a lot of muttered cursing, I finally replaced and reconnected the wires, cogs, and rusted-out pins. I then worked on the automaton's joints, brushing out rust and oiling all of her parts. It took me the better part of two hours. Once I felt sure she was repaired as much as I could do, I tidied up her clothes and got her ready. Then, I considered what to do. I didn't have her key. Now, I'd have to discover just how much I'd trespassed.

I turned Mister Flint's windup key, switching the mechanical back on.

A series of clicks emanated form his chest, and he slowly came back to life.

"Mister Flint, are you all right?" I asked, extending a hand to help him sit up.

"Yes, yes. I think so. Good to shut down for a bit. Restful."

"I think the knee is repaired. Shall we give it a try? Easy

standing up," I said, taking both of his hands. Again, to my surprise, his metal was warm to the touch.

He nodded then rose slowly.

Guiding him, I helped him take a couple of steps. The knee bent perfectly.

"Miss Hawking! You clever tinker, you have it! I can't believe you—" He stopped cold when he saw the maid standing by the window.

"I...I was looking in the closet for a magnifying glass when I found her. I hope it's okay. I worked on her a bit. I believe she's repaired now. I just didn't have her key to test her."

Mister Flint turned and looked at me, his optics spinning. "She's repaired?" I could hear the surprise in his voice.

"I believe so, but I will need her key to restart her."

"Miss Hawking, are you quite serious? You've repaired her?"

"I think so. I wasn't able to get a look at the cogs inside her head, but I was able to replace her core wires and refresh her joints. It looked like she got wet. Is that right?"

"Yes. She was caught in the rain and shorted," Mister Flint said then turned and picked up his jacket. From an interior pocket, he pulled out a key and handed it to me. He then slipped his shirt and coat back on as he watched me.

Taking the windup key, I went to the mech and slipped her key inside the keyhole. It took several cranks to wind her. When I was done, I removed the key and stepped back.

From deep within the automaton, I heard a series of clicking sounds. This was followed by a series of brief and halting movements as each limb seemed to come back to life. I heard the automaton's optics spin, then she turned and looked from Mister Flint to me. She attempted to say something, but it took a moment for her voice box to work. When she did speak, her words puzzled me.

"You. It's you. Mister Flint, it's her," the automaton

exclaimed, gesturing to me. "But…but if it's her, why am I still like this?"

"Oh my dear Bronwyn, it's so good to have you back," Mister Flint said, ignoring the question as he embraced the automaton. "Your mother has missed you so."

"Mother?" I asked.

"Oh. Yes. Missus Silver is like a mother to her, you see," Mister Flint said, then a series of loud clicks emitted from his chest. The maid tilted her head as if to listen, and then she clicked in reply. Mister Flint answered her with another series of clicks.

I frowned at Mister Flint. "It's rude to talk behind my back."

Once again, I felt his embarrassment. "Oh! I'm very sorry, Miss Hawking. Yes, you're quite right."

"Mistress, you repaired me? The last thing I remember was coming back from the beach, the rain, and then…nothing."

"You broke down, my dear. Miss Hawking has fixed you."

The automaton curtseyed to me. "Thank you, mistress."

"Look," Mister Flint said, pointing out the window. Rhys and Missus Silver were walking back toward the castle door. I noticed that Rhys carried a small chest in one hand and hoisted an umbrella in the other. Missus Silver also carried an umbrella. A soft rain continued to fall.

Without another word, the maid turned and ran out of the room.

"Bronwyn, go slowly. Bronwyn, be careful," Mister Flint called, rushing behind her, me rushing behind him. "I say, Miss Hawking, you've done a splendid job with this knee. Thank you."

"You're very welcome."

Rushing behind the mechanicals, I reached the foyer just as Missus Silver and Rhys stepped inside.

"Mother," Bronwyn yelled and ran to Missus Silver.

Rhys stiffened, a look of surprise on his face. He stared at Bronwyn, who was hugging Missus Silver, then looked from Mister Flint to me.

"Mister Flint?" he asked.

"My lord, it's all Miss Hawking's doing. Quite by accident, she discovered Bronwyn in the workshop—we'd gone there to see about my knee—and she made a full repair!"

"Oh, my dear! Oh, my dear," Missus Silver said, holding the other automaton tightly. Tears of oil trailed down the automaton's cheeks.

The scene startled me. This was beyond the capacity of ethics boards, aether cores, or other clockworks. This was so much more.

Kelly jumped excitedly all around the mechanical.

The maid paused and petted the dog.

"And how are you feeling?" Missus Silver asked Bronwyn. "Is everything working all right?"

"I...I think so. Some of the gears are still a little stiff, but the oil is working its way through, loosening things up."

Missus Silver left the young mechanical then crossed the room and wrapped her arms around me. Her body felt stiff, metallic under her worn gown, but there was a *feeling* of pure joy radiating from her. "Thank you, Miss Hawking."

"Of course."

"Master," the girl said meekly, carefully embracing Rhys, who gave her quick and polite embrace.

"We've missed you, Bronwyn," he told her then turned to me. "I'm in your debt," he said, bowing to me.

"Think nothing of it," I said then smiled at the mechanicals.

"Oh, you must excuse us, Miss Hawking. We need to find Mister Steele and Missus Smith and share the good news."

"And have you seen my knee?" Mister Flint said, following behind the two female automatons as they headed down the hallway in the direction of the kitchen. "It bends perfectly. It didn't even work this well before."

"What a blessed day," Missus Silver said. "Let's hope more blessings come our way," she called over her shoulder, looking toward Rhys.

He chuckled lightly.

"They are very attached to one another," I said as I watched them go.

Rhys nodded. "Yes. I must thank you again. You have done us a great favor."

"You're very welcome," I said then looked down at my hands which were now covered in gear grease and rust. "Oh dear. If you'll excuse me, I think I need to wash up."

To my surprise, Rhys reached out and gently touched the bruise on my arm. It had turned an angry shade of purple with yellow around the edges of the bruise.

"Please know how very sorry I am. I am mortified to see you in such a condition."

I looked up at the mechanical. A strange feeling swelled in my stomach as I took in the expression on his face. He looked so terribly sad. His plight moved me.

"None of us are without imperfections," I said. "It was an accident, and you are forgiven."

"Thank you, Miss Hawking."

I nodded then turned and headed up the stairs toward my bedchamber.

"Miss Hawking?" Rhys called from behind me.

"Yes?"

"Do you like music?"

"Music? Of course."

"Excellent," Rhys said then bowed to me. He turned and followed the other automatons to the kitchen.

Feeling confused, I headed back upstairs. My heart was beating hard, and there was a swelling feeling in my chest. I was so thrilled to have helped Bronwyn and Mister Flint. And it pleased me to no end to see Missus Silver so happy. But more than that, Rhys's happiness moved me more than it should, more than reason dictated. He was just a machine, right? He was just a machine. And if he was nothing more than analytics and ethics boards, cogs, gears, and wires, then why did I feeling *something* for him?

But I did.

And the thought terrified me.

25
A TALE AS OLD AS TIME

ALONE IN MY CHAMBER, I WASHED UP THEN LOCKED THE door and sat down on my bed. I pulled the yellowed letters from my pocket.

The first letter to Lord Rhys Llewellyn detailed supplies that would be sent from Wales to the castle in the coming months. A rich bounty of wines, meats, textiles, and even livestock was detailed. The bill, it seemed, had already been paid in full. But what was of interest to me was the date: 1726. Almost one hundred years ago. I stared at the name on the paper: Lord Rhys Llewellyn. Had the lord named his automaton after himself? I also noted that nowhere in that supply list did I see any indication of supplies of a clockwork sort.

I thumbed to the next letter, which had from Master Archibald Boatswain. As Papa had rightly guessed, the famed inventor had been connected to this place. His message was brief, indicating that he planned to come with his "little gift" in the coming weeks. The tone of the letter was very familiar, as if he and the lord—now, was it Lord Rhys the elder or the boy in the painting—were friends.

I set the letter aside and opened the final piece of mail. This message was far more formal in nature. It had come from a silver mining company in England. It detailed the plans, down to the number of laborers, pieces of equipment, and tools that would be brought to the Isle of Annwfn for work and construction of the Annwfn mine.

I stared at the letter. A silver mine. That's what I'd discovered? I frowned. Then why the secrecy?

There was a knock at the door. "Miss Hawking?" Missus Silver called.

I shoved the letters under my pillow then rose to answer the door. "Yes?" I replied, opening the door.

Missus Silver entered carrying my yellow ball gown. "I took the liberty of washing it. It's been drying by the fire. I had to mend a few spots, but the dress is all back in order. Lord Rhys... Lord Rhys would like to do something special to thank you for restoring Bronwyn to us. He has a dinner and some music planned if you will join him. A formal affair. I'd love to see you in this gown, my dear."

"A formal dinner?"

"Yes."

"And music?"

"Yes. In our ballroom."

"You have a ballroom?"

"Indeed we do. The most beautiful ballroom in all of Wales. Do you accept Lord Rhys's invitation?"

"I... Of course."

"Very good," Missus Silver said then turned to go.

"Missus Silver," I called. "You refer to the automaton as Lord Rhys, the same name as the owner of this castle."

Missus Silver's lids lifted, her optics shining brightly. She smiled. "Yes, I do," she said then turned and left, leaving me to stare at the door in her wake.

My HANDS SHOOK NERVOUSLY as I slid on the yellow ball gown. It was quite silly, really, feeling so nervous. What was there to be worried about? I had done something to help the mechanicals, and they found a way to thank me the best they knew how.

Adjusting the dress, I sat down and looked into the vanity mirror. I smoothed my hair back once more. I'd styled it as Elyse Murray often wore her hair. Then I adjusted the small bumblebee hairpin in my hair—its cousin gifted to the fairies. I dabbed some perfume on my neck. By now, the Scottish lord who Papa and I had traveled to meet was already married. I'd missed that wedding. The ball gown was going to go to waste. At the very least, I would enjoy dressing up for just one night.

I adjusted the off-the-shoulder sleeves of my dress then pulled on my long, yellow gloves. Even my pair of heeled silk dancing slippers had survived in the box. I was suddenly very grateful for them. It would not do to wear traveling boots under a ball gown.

I took a deep breath, steadied my nerve, then rose and headed to the stairwell.

To my surprise, all of the candelabras in the main foyer had been lit, even the massive chandelier that hung overhead. The hall, which had seemed so dim before, was bathed in orange light. Everything felt so cheery and alive.

At the bottom of the stairs, Mister Flint, Missus Silver, Bronwyn, Missus Smith, the cook, and Mister Steele, another of the servants, stood waiting. All of them were dressed in their finest. It pleased me to see Missus Silver with her arm wrapped around Bronwyn's waist.

And alongside them was Rhys, who was dressed in a handsome suit. He wore a dark blue doublet trimmed with gold embroidery, a white silk collar, breeches and leggings, and boots. His metallic face glimmered as if it had been polished.

My stomach rocked with butterflies the size of ravens.

Isabelle, you're being ridiculous. He's just a machine.

When I reached the bottom of the stairs, the ladies curt-seyed, the men bowed.

Rhys offered his arm.

I linked my arm with his, and we moved down the hallway opposite that which led to the library. At the end of this hall was a set of double doors.

Mister Flint opened the doors to reveal a massive ballroom.

The place was bathed in light. The hardwood floor made of a light-colored timber gleamed. The walls were painted white and fixed with gold sconces and trim. A table had been set up for dinner. On the table were vases of wildflowers.

Rhys pulled out a chair for me, but I paused a moment when I spotted a piano sitting in the corner.

"Is that a pneumatic piano?" I asked, staring at the rare music piece.

"It is. It was a gift from Master Boatswain," Rhys replied.

"Archibald Boatswain?"

Rhys nodded. "He was a friend...to this house."

"I..." I said, looking from my seat at the dinner table to the piano. It was such a rare piece. "Do you mind if I—"

Rhys laughed. "Please, go ahead. You won't be able to eat a bite until your curiosity is sated."

"The music boxes I design... I studied all of Boatswain's musical creations to understand how to make the metallic rollers to produce sound. I read that he had designed a few pianos, but no one knew what happened to them. Does it really play multiple songs?"

"Indeed it does." Rhys went behind the piano and opened a panel. First, he pumped a pedal at the back to build air pressure. He then activated a lever inside. Once he'd done so, he slowly let his foot off the pedal.

The gears inside the machine turned, and a moment later, the mechanics began to work.

I gasped as the music sounded from the piano. A moment later, the entire ballroom was bathed in the dulcet notes of a waltz.

I looked at Rhys, my eyes wide with excitement.

He extended his hand. I couldn't help but notice it was the hand I had repaired. "A dance?"

I nodded then set my hand in his.

Rhys led me to the center of the room. Gently setting his other hand on my waist, he led me into a waltz.

I was suddenly very glad that Papa had made me practice dancing in the months leading up to the trip. It was Papa who had to endure the injured toes. While I was not an accomplished dancer by any stretch of the imagination, I could manage. I smiled. Was I a refined lady? No. That was not me. Mechanically skilled? Yes. Clever? Yes. I was well read and not bad looking. But refined? Well, no, but at the very least, I was able to pull off the waltz.

As Rhys and I spun around the room, however, I took a bit of pride in myself. Clearly, he knew all the forms of formal dance. He moved with precision. I was happy that I could keep step and was even more pleased to see a joyful look on Rhys's mechanical face. How unlikely it seemed that a metallic man could express so much emotion.

He looked truly glad.

And when he gazed at me, he looked…well, now I was just reading into things. An automaton could not fall in love. Right? Right? But that look… He seemed enamored. And more, I sensed deep emotion in his expression which moved me.

The notes from the player piano filled the room with sweet music.

We paused when the song ended. I glanced back at the piano, curious to see how the machine would shift to the next piece. I smiled at Rhys then went back to the piano. Through the pane of glass above the keys, I watched as the metallic drum rolled. The metal had been beaten as thin as paper. A new roll of metal moved onto the player and the second song started. I stared at the machine. Boatswain had tinkered the material with the craft of a master metallurgist and the precision of a surgeon. He was a true master.

"It's amazing," I whispered, touching the glass.

"I'm glad it pleases you. Are you hungry?"

I nodded then Rhys and I both took a seat at the dining table. I ate quickly and lightly, well-aware that Rhys was not eating, as we chatted about the inner workings of the pneumatic piano. The servants had outdone themselves in preparing the meal: broiled lobster tail, truffles, puréed quince, baked garlic, and bara brith. Everything was delicious. As soon as I was done, I rose once more and went to the piano in time to see the roller move to another song. This time, the piano played Vivaldi.

"So someone else here was a lover of Vivaldi's works," I said.

"Indeed," Rhys replied then extended his hand to me.

Again, we took to the floor. We moved slowly, spinning around the room with gentle ease. I loved the feel of my gown, the sweep of it as the hem brushed the floor, and the sensation of Rhys's hand on my hip. I smiled at him. If only he were a living man. If only he were flesh and blood. If only he were the man I had seen in the enchanted mirror.

Rhys spun me once more, lowering me into a dip. When he gently lifted me, our eyes met. The expression on his face surprised me. If he'd been a living man, I'd swear he wanted to kiss me.

"Isabelle," he whispered, touching my cheek gently. "There's something I must tell you."

My heart beat hard in my chest.

You cannot possibly be falling in love with an automaton.

This isn't happening.

This can't be happening.

"Rhys," I whispered.

"Isabelle, I…" he began then leaned toward me.

I froze, knowing the kiss was coming, not sure what to do, but wanting it all the same.

The piano suddenly clanked loudly. There was a sharp whine and then a loud pop followed by the shattering of glass.

Rhys stilled and looked toward the piano.

My breath quick, I suddenly caught hold of my senses.

The ballroom door handle rattled.

Both Rhys and I stepped away from one another.

The door opened, and Mister Flint entered. "Lord Rhys, is everything all right? Oh my dear, what has happened to Master Boatswain's piano?"

Rhys and I crossed the room to look at the instrument. Heavy tension filled the air, unspoken words, unspoken deeds.

And at the heart of that was my confused emotions.

"Let me clean up the glass before Miss Hawking gets hurt," Mister Flint said then hurried back into the hallway to fetch a broom.

Moving carefully around the glass, I looked inside the piano. "It became misaligned. There," I said, pointing to the place where the rolled metal had gone astray. I traced the lines with my eyes. "Ah, I see. Look. The lead rusted off." I went around to the back of the piano and removed the panel. Pulling off my yellow gloves, I knelt down then leaned into the instrument, looking at the broken piece. I inspected the inner workings. "Nothing else is broken save the glass and the rusted lead. Once the piece is replaced, it will work again. The lead has an odd shape though. It will need smithing to make a new one."

I crawled back out of the instrument and dusted off my hands and dress.

"I...I do apologize," Rhys said, his voice sounding tepid and awkward. "It has worked these many years. I'm sorry that it chose tonight to malfunction."

"We all malfunction at times. And it does seem that the timing is never right. I did enjoy the music and the dancing. I loved all of it. Thank you, Rhys," I said, perfectly aware that he was going to tell me something essential before Master Boatswain's design decided to interrupt. And maybe more. The thought that the mechanical wanted to kiss me confused me.

Rhys bowed. "Thank you for joining me. It was a great pleasure."

I stared at him. Whatever he was going to say, it appeared he'd decided it was better not to say anything.

The clock in the hall chimed ten o'clock.

"It's very late. I'm sorry to have you up so long. You must be tired after today's long walk," Rhys said.

I wasn't tired, but he already knew that.

"Rhys?"

"If you want to retire, please don't stay up on my account. Mister Flint and I will work on cleaning up the piano."

"I... All right. I do thank you for everything," I said, searching his metallic face. Strange mech, what was he playing at? "It was an enchanting evening."

At first Rhys avoided my glance, but then he turned and looked at me. He looked so sad. "It was my pleasure, Miss Hawking. More than you can ever know."

A wash of mixed emotions nagged at me. I felt scared, sad, anxious, and...and a new feeling bloomed inside of me that I simply could not accept. He was a machine. This couldn't be happening.

I curtseyed to him.

He bowed politely in reply.

Then I turned and left the ballroom. I headed down the hall, crossed the foyer, and went outside to the metallic garden. I walked away from the castle until I found my way to a bench. Only there, once I was able to sit down in the darkness, out of sight of everyone, did I allow myself to cry.

26
TYLWYTH TEG

ISABELLE.

Wiping the hot tears from my eyes, I turned and looked east toward the dark forest.

Isabelle, come.

Rising, I looked back at the castle. I saw candlelight through the windows, but no one had come outside.

Inhaling deeply, I walked through the garden to the east gate. To my surprise, the ornate gate was open. I stared down the path. For some reason, I wasn't surprised to see a row of glowing blue mushrooms leading away from the castle.

I looked back at the fortress once more.

What was he going to tell me?

Was he really going to kiss me?

Was I losing my mind?

Isabelle, come.

My hands shaking, I stepped out into the dark forest, following the trail of fungi. I didn't need them. I knew where I was going. I'd known it since I first set eyes on the place. The trail would lead me to the cave.

Slim beams of moonlight guided my path as I worked my way down the road back to the trail that led to the mine.

Feeling my ankle twist as I stepped on yet another rock, I grumbled, "Stupid shoes." I stopped and pulled off the delicate silk and bejeweled heels. As I turned down the side path leading to the mine, I set the shoes on a small boulder so I'd easily find them again. Steeling my nerve, I walked barefoot toward the mine.

The sounds of night birds and insects made a chorus in the dark forest. As I walked, my eyes adjusted to the dim light, and I made out shapes on the forest floor, including the fallen standing stone lying underneath the timbers of the cut tree. Under the light of the moon, it cast a soft blue glow.

I walked up the small hill to the entrance of the cave.

Moonbeams illuminated the entrance. Inside, it was as dark as a tomb. A lantern hung just inside. I grabbed the lamp then felt the shelf above it for matches. Although it was covered in dirt and cobwebs, I found a flint box. I lit the lantern. The orange glow of the flame seemed gaudy under the silvery moonlight. Standing at the mouth of the cave, mindful of every fairy tale and goblin story I had ever read or heard, I entered slowly. The answer to the mystery was here. And tonight, I would find it.

I followed the rail line deep into the cave. It was clear that blasting and mining had destroyed the natural splendor of this place. I walked through the darkness, feeling the angle of the rail line—and the cave—descend. I followed the metal rail until it reached its end at a natural slant in the rock. Here, the mine had not been blasted. Veins of silver still streaked the cave walls. It was beautiful. It glowed under the light of the lantern. The company had come this far, but no further. Ahead of me, the direction of the cave shifted dramatically to the left. A slim passage moved deeper into the cave. Above this entrance, I saw the same markings.

Isabelle. Come.

The voice, like a soft whisper, breathed from inside the dark cave. But this time, I could tell the voice was distinctly feminine, and the owner was close by.

Inhaling deeply, I steadied myself then pushed forward. The passage was long, narrow, and tilted to the side. Here, as in the other cave, silver veins marked the walls. I moved through the passage, exiting into a vast cavern.

I gasped. The walls all around glimmered with silver. The metal appeared like ivy, twisting through the rocks. Stalactites and stalagmites of silver protruded from the ceiling and floor. In the center of the room was a pool of water that glowed blue, the depths below shining incandescently.

Sitting at the water's edge, her fingertips gently brushing the water's surface, was the most beautiful woman I had ever seen.

"Hello, Isabelle," she whispered, her voice tinkling like a silver bell.

I set the lamp down. The blue hue coming off the water was all the light I needed. I stared at the woman. Her hair was silvery in color, as were her eyes. She wore a soft blue dress embroidered all along the edges with silver thread in the shape of oak leaves, acorns, birds, and flowers. On her head was a silver diadem with a rainbow-colored gem at the middle.

"How do you like my forest?" she asked.

Her voice had a strange hollow sound, tinny and ethereal all at once.

"Beautiful. The most beautiful forest I have ever seen."

"And my standing stones? I've seen you looking at them,

studying them, trying to discover their secrets. Do you like them as well?"

"I do," I said carefully, fully aware that my skin had risen to gooseflesh, the hairs on the back of my neck standing up. Something inside me was screaming at me to run.

"They are very old, as are the symbols thereon. I like that you find them curious. I see you have a sharp mind. Do you like my island?"

"I do."

"And what about the castle grounds, do you like the *perfect* garden?"

I could feel the trap in the question. "I… It is an interesting puzzle."

The woman laughed, but not menacingly. "And what about the castle? Do you like it?"

My heart was slamming in my chest. I had been wrong to come here. I was in terrible danger. One wrong answer, and I would pay dearly. "I like the library."

Again, she laughed. "And what about the little toy soldiers inside?"

I stared at her. She was smirking now. There was so much malice in the expression, I was taken aback.

I didn't answer.

"I like my forest, my stones, my cave," she said, motioning about her. "I suppose I might even like that library you mention, though I have not seen it. I didn't mind the castle much, not when the lady lived there. I liked her very much, her paintings, even her little hermitage which I permitted. I even enjoyed her boy, when he was young and full of his own will. Such a lively, happy thing, full of art and life. Funny how all things transform with time. But I hated that garden. The bramble, the flowers, they all wept from the constant cutting and pruning and shaping and molding. Perfect lines. Perfect shapes. I hated it, but I even let that pass."

She stared at me. "You are an interesting thing. You have the mind of a tinker but the heart of my people. Why do you like my forest?"

"For its natural grace."

"Natural grace. Like that?" she said, motioning across the cave. There, amongst a stack of other riches, sat my sculpture of the birds who sang Vivaldi.

I gasped. "H-how?"

The woman waved her hand and the music box sprang to life, the little birds warbling perfectly. She waved her hand once more, stopping the tune, then turned back to me.

"You, who can create that, must understand what I have done here, why I have done it. I could not have them take this place from us, you see? Do you understand? The old lord was a man of coin and when he died, we all rejoiced. But the young lord, whom we all loved, changed. He wanted to live up to his father's reputation. He wanted his father's wealth and fame. So he came here, sketched and planned, then brought machines. Here. To this sacred place where his mother had warned him never to tread. Where his mother had told him that we still existed. Where we had taken sanctuary. He came here to destroy what was left. I could not let him, you must understand. I could not let him become a man of metal, a man of machines, a man without the heart that his mother had nurtured in him. I could not let him take this place from us. So I gave him what he wanted. I wanted him to see what it meant to be a man of metal. I made him, all of them, and that accursed garden, exactly what they were all trying to be.

"I gave them what they wanted to show them.

"To teach them.

"To punish them.

"Do you understand?"

I did understand. I truly and clearly understood. Rhys and the others were not machines. They were living people turned clockwork by this fey creature. I did understand, but I did not approve.

"How could you do such a thing?" I retorted hotly, instantly regretting my tone.

The fey woman's face darkened. "He deserved it. He wanted to be a man of metal, he wanted to rape this place to make his fortune. Well, I made him into what he wanted. I thought you would understand."

"I understand why you did it. This place is special, sacred. I see that. But what of Rhys? Did you ever seek him out, show him, ask him to stop?"

"His heart was corrupted by his father. He loved nothing, no one, save wealth and luxury. He became a hard man in spirit, so I made him so in flesh."

"That's not true."

"No? I see that bruise on your arm, Isabelle Hawking. The lord is still a monster, and a monster he will remain until he learns to love and is worthy of another's love. But rusted toys can never be repaired," she said with a laugh. "Rusted toys can never be healed. Don't you see? There is no hope. There is no key to that heart. No key!" she said and then began laughing loudly and menacingly.

Her laughter, however, was cut short by the sound of barking.

Kelly.

The fey creature rose with fierce suddenness. Her eyes turned black, her face contorting angrily as she glared at the cave opening.

"Leave this place," she hissed at me.

"Isabelle?" Rhys called from the cave.

"Rhys," I yelled in reply.

I turned to look back at the fey woman then gasped to find her at my side. Her gown flowed unnaturally all around her.

Her eyes were black as coal, her silver hair flying as if caught in a torrent.

"Leave. Leave this place. Leave this island and never come back. I was wrong. He does not deserve your love. He does not deserve to feel again. Leave this place and let him rust as punishment for seeking to destroy the last sanctuary of my kind," she said. Then, in a flurry of skirts, she disappeared into the pool of water.

The cave rumbled, rocks tumbling in an alcove not far away.

"Isabelle? Isabelle, where are you?" Rhys called.

The cave shook once more. Rocks tumbled from the ceiling, crashing down on the lantern.

Kelly appeared at the entrance of the cave and barked loudly. I raced to her.

"Come on, Kelly. Let's go," I said. I moved quickly, working my way as fast as I could through the narrow passage.

"Isabelle?"

The cave shook again. I put my hands over my head, fending off the falling rocks. My eyes adjusted to the darkness, and in the distance, I made out the light of Rhys's optics.

"Rhys? Rhys, I'm coming."

Kelly raced ahead.

I stepped out of the narrow passage as the cave shook once more.

"Rhys," I said, reaching out for him, reaching out and knowing that the strange metal man for whom I had a growing attachment was no automaton at all. He was a real man cursed by a faerie. "Rhys."

But then something overhead let loose, and a moment later, everything went dark.

27
SAY SOMETHING

VOICES DRIFTED TO MY EARS EVEN BEFORE I OPENED my eyes.

I heard Papa.

And...Gerard?

Why was Gerard at our workshop? Don't tell me Papa was actually considering him as a suitor for me. I'd need to explain to Papa that I had a growing attachment for...

"Rhys." I sat upright, my eyes flying open.

"Easy, Miss Hawking. Easy. You took another blow to the head. Some rubble fell on you, as I understand it. My dear, I don't think our island is very good for your health."

I looked around the room. I was in my chamber at the castle once more. I stared at the door and listened. I did hear Papa. And Gerard.

"Missus Silver..."

"Your father is here. And another London gentleman—so to speak. There is an airship docked in front of the castle. They arrived this morning."

"Missus Silver, where is Rhys? I must speak with him at once."

"Bronwyn, dear. Please fetch the master. Miss Hawking, shall I send for your father as well?"

I bit my lip. "No. Not yet."

I stared out the window. The sky was sunny and bright. It was a perfect day for flying.

No.

Not now.

Not yet.

My head ached. I lifted my hand to my forehead, where I felt a bandage.

Missus Silver busied herself nervously as we both waited. After a moment, I realized she was packing my things.

Heavy footsteps rushed down the hall. A moment later, Rhys appeared at the door.

"My lord, she just woke," Missus Silver said as she set the stack of books on the Greek inventors into a piece of luggage. She'd also packed up all my sketches and my silk dancing slippers. My yellow gown hung by the wardrobe. From the sweet smell of soap that perfumed the air, I could tell all my clothes had been freshly laundered. Missus Silver had prepared everything for me to leave.

Missus Silver passed the lord, gave him a knowing glance, then closed the door behind her.

"Please, come sit," I said, patting the bed beside me.

"Are you... How are you feeling?" he asked. Adjusting the tails on his jacket, he sat.

"My head aches."

"The cave started to collapse. A rock fell on you. I was able to get us out in time. Isabelle, what were you thinking going there?"

"I was thinking...that it was time for me to learn the truth."

"The truth?"

"Yes."

"And…did you learn the truth?"

I slid my hand into his. The feel of his fingers, warm as flesh but hard as metal, made me sad beyond all measure. I stroked my finger over his, feeling the pins and bearings at his joints, the gears that worked the hand. A tear slipped down my cheek. "Yes. Rhys…why didn't you tell me?"

"Who would believe such a story?"

"Such a terrible curse. The fey woman… Her punishment was beyond reason."

"No. She was right. I lost my way."

"But this? And not just you, the others too. What was their crime? They didn't bring the mining company here."

"No. They did not. I did. I am the one who knowingly disrupted that sacred place. And I'm paying the price. But it will be over soon. My heart," he said, touching his chest. "There is no windup key for me. My heart is winding down. Each day it becomes a little harder. Soon, I will be done, and when I pass, the others will be restored."

"Your windup key… Where is it?"

Rhys laughed. "Every day a chest appears at the castle gate. She told me when she cast this curse upon me that when I learned my lesson, I would be given my key. Every day a case of keys arrives. Every day I try them. None of them ever fits."

I remembered the faerie woman's horrible words. She had said there was no key, no hope.

"I will make you a key," I said. "I will make you a key. That, at least, I *can* fix."

Rhys shook his head. "No. No, you will let it go. You will return to London with your father and the gentleman downstairs who informs me he's planning to marry you. You will return to London, and you will forget me. Let my heart stop. At least I can free the others from this curse."

"But Rhys, you must at least let me try. I cannot bear the

thought of you—of your heart stopping." Another tear trickled down my cheek.

Rhys reached out and wiped it away. "You must. It is too late for me."

"No. No, it's not," I whispered, unable to find a way to make him understand. The faerie woman had said that if he learned to love another, and if someone shared that love, the curse could be broken. But how could I say that to him? How could I tell him that if he just went ahead and loved me, all would be healed? I could not force him to love me no matter how attached I felt to him.

"It is. Please, Isabelle. Please return to London and forget me."

I reached out and touched his cheek. "Can you feel my touch?"

"No, not as I did when I was living flesh."

I sighed. "I will return to London on one condition."

Rhys's optics turned as he studied me. "And that is?"

"That you let me take an imprint of your heart. I will take the imprint, return to London, and make you a key. I will make it, and I will come back."

"And the gentleman below—the one who claims he will marry you—why would he ever permit you to return? Or your father, who in my haste to get him away from this terrible place, I treated so unkindly?"

I laughed. "First, Gerard is quite mistaken. I will never marry him. And second, my father will forgive you when he understands what has happened."

At that, Rhys seemed to brighten. He scanned my face, but then his expression fell into shadow once more. "I will let you make the imprint if it means you will go. You are too full of life for this place. Don't try to come back."

I rose and went to the writing desk. Grabbing a slip of

paper and a bottle of ink, I turned and faced him. "I need you to lie down."

"Isabelle," he began in protest.

"If you want me to leave, do as I ask."

"It's not that I *want* you to leave, it's just—"

"Do as I ask, you stubborn man."

Rhys laughed. "At least now you know I *am* a man," he said then lay down.

"Beastly, though," I said with a grin.

"Yes, I have been. I admit. And I am sorry."

I sat down beside him. I reached out for his shirt then paused. "I… I will need to see."

"All right."

My hands trembling, I untied his collar then unbuttoned his shirt. The body below was made entirely of metal. His chest had been shaped in the form of a man's, but under his pectoral muscles and ribs, it was open to reveal the clockwork mechanisms inside. I swallowed hard, grief nearly over-whelming me when I saw.

"Isabelle," he whispered.

A tear streamed down my cheek. I shook my head. "I'll fix this. I'll make the key and come back for you."

On his chest was a silver piece of metal shaped like a heart. There, I found a small keyhole. His windup key was not like the others. First, it was not on his back. Second, the shape of it was unusual.

Folding the piece of paper so it could slip inside the keyhole, I carefully poured a few drops of ink then slid the paper inside the opening. I concentrated hard as I leaned over Rhys. I needed to get the imprint just right.

"Does it hurt?" I whispered as I worked.

"It feels…strange." He reached out and touched my hair with his other hand. "I can't really feel your hair. I feel the sensation of something there, but not the feel of a beautiful woman's locks."

His voice sounded so forlorn that it nearly broke my heart. I choked back the sob. Working carefully, ensuring I got a good imprint, I put pressure on the paper within. Then, I pulled the paper back out. I studied the design on the paper.

"The key is grooved at the bottom," I said. "Unless the grooves are right, a regular key will never work. Rhys, I'll return in a week. I promise you."

"Please, Isabelle. You promised."

"I promised I would leave. I didn't promise I wouldn't come back."

Rhys took my hand then and looked up at me. His optics turned, his lids low. He reached out and stroked my face once more. "I'm sorry that I cannot truly feel your skin."

"Don't give up hope," I whispered.

The door handle rattled.

"Sir, please. Your daughter asked for a moment," Missus Silver was saying.

"Isabelle?" Papa called, pushing the door open. "Isabelle?"

Rhys pulled his hand back, but I didn't let go of him.

"I'm here, Papa."

My father rounded the side of my bed to find Rhys lying there. Had he not been an automaton—at least in my father's eyes, for the time being—the situation would have looked rather compromising. As it was, I felt a blush rise to my cheeks.

Rhys sat up. "Thank you, Miss Hawking," he said then began buttoning his shirt.

I rose to embrace my father, tucking the print of the key into my sleeve.

"Isabelle. Oh, my sweet girl. They told me you were hurt in a mine collapse," my father said aghast. "I saw you earlier today, but you were still asleep." Papa reached out and lightly touched the bandage on my forehead. "My poor girl."

"She should see a doctor as soon as she returns to

London," Rhys said, standing once more. He adjusted his coat and stood in a formal posture, his hands behind his back. "With the injury during the shipwreck, and now this, she needs a formal evaluation."

"Yes, of course," my father said dismissively. "Are you well enough to fly? The airship crew is waiting, and Gerard is here with me."

"So I understand. Papa, why is Gerard here?"

My father laughed. "My girl, no one was able to help me discover the location of this island except Gerard. He had an ancient map, taken from the Roman account of the invasion of Britain, which marked the place. From that, he determined the island's location. He is a clever man. And he was very concerned for you. You know, Isabelle, I do believe he genuinely cares—"

"Now is not the time, Papa," I said, glancing back at Rhys.

"Yes. Yes. You're quite right. Very well, then. Let's have your things taken to the airship, and we shall leave this place at once."

Standing by the door, Missus Silver choked back a little sob.

"I… Give me just a moment, Papa. I'll have them bring the case down. I just need to change."

"Very good. Oh, my Isabelle. I am so relieved. I shall get you home, and we will never leave London again!" Papa said, pinching my cheek. Then he turned and headed back out.

"Miss… Miss Hawking, shall I take your things down-stairs?" Missus Silver asked, her voice unsteady. "I left your traveling dress in the wardrobe. The only thing left to pack is the gown."

"Please leave it here."

"Leave it here?"

"Yes, for when I return."

Something inside Missus Silver clicked quickly and happily.

"Of course, Miss Hawking," she said then closed up the case. Casting a glance to Rhys and me, she grabbed the suitcase then left us alone.

"I should... I'll go so you can change," Rhys said.

I nodded, unsure what else I could say. I didn't know whether or not Rhys cared for me as I had grown to care for him. My heart beat hard as I sought for the right words. There was something between us, wasn't there? He felt it too, didn't he? But I had been wrong about Doctor Murray. Maybe I was wrong about Rhys too.

Rhys stayed a moment longer. It seemed to me he was also searching for the right words, but in the end, he went to the door.

"Rhys," I whispered, tears trailing down my cheeks. "I will come back for you."

He stared at the door a moment then turned and looked back at me. "I hope you can. But I fear I will never see you again," he said then left.

28
INTO THE CLOUDS

IT WAS STARTLING TO SEE THE AIRSHIP HOVERING OVER THE metallic garden. The crew, who seemed content to mind their own business, waited patiently for us to depart.

"Isabelle, are you well enough to climb the ladder? I can have them prepare a stretcher to lift you," Gerard said, his voice full of what seemed like legitimate concern.

"I… No, I'll be fine. Thank you."

"May I take your satchel?"

I unstrung my bag and handed it to him. "Thank you."

Gerard beamed at me then turned and climbed up the rope ladder to the airship. The rest of my belongings, it seemed, had already been loaded.

I looked at Papa. "Is the climb all right for you?"

"I'll manage it, my girl. I was climbing in and out of these machines before you were born. I must say, the relic I flew home in held up well. I have taken it to the London Tinker's Society headquarters. The Rude Mechanicals have expressed an interest in the machine. Was the ship really designed by Master Boatswain?" my father asked Rhys.

Rhys nodded. "Master Boatswain was a friend of the lord

of this castle. It was a gift. It is yours to do with as you wish, Master Hawking."

"Very good. Very good. My thanks," my father said then leaned in toward me. "Did you work on his analytics?"

I looked at Rhys who was smiling softly.

"In a way," I replied.

Rhys chuckled.

Kelly trotted over to me. She pawed my leg gently.

"Stay away from the selkies while I'm gone," I told her, setting my hand on her head. I went to embrace Missus Silver who was holding back a sob.

"Please, Missus Silver, don't get upset. You may overtax your core again."

She nodded. "We shall miss you," she told me, gently touching on my cheek.

"Please, don't worry. I'll be back soon," I said, hugging her once more.

"Thank you for all you did for me, mistress," Bronwyn added, placing her hand on my arm.

"It was my pleasure," I replied.

Missus Smith and Master Lucas were also there. I curtseyed to them then turned to Mister Flint.

"Thank you for taking care of me," I told Mister Flint who also seemed upset.

"It was my pleasure, Miss Hawking. You brought life to this old, tired place. I hope we see you again."

"You will."

I nodded to Papa.

He headed toward the rope ladder and began the climb up.

Rhys walked with me to the ladder. When we arrived, he took hold of the rope. "I'll steady it for you."

"Rhys…"

He looked down at me, a soft smile on his face. "Farewell, Isabelle Hawking. It was…an honor to meet you."

"Remember what I told you. I will come back. Soon."

He smiled lightly then steadied the ladder.

I inhaled deeply then grabbed on. It wasn't a far climb, but in my fragile state, it winded me all the same. By the time I reached the airship's gondola, I felt dizzy. Papa and Gerard reached out, helping me aboard.

The airship crew got to work hoisting the ladder and readying the balloon. I went to the side of the ship and looked over. Below, the automatons waved goodbye. Rhys stood slightly aside from the others, Kelly at his side.

A soft wind blew in from the forest. The ship lifted. The rudder at the back of the ship clicked on and the prow of the ship turned to the east.

I went to the back of the ship and stood at the stern. Waving, I watched as their figures became smaller and smaller as the airship lifted higher.

Soon, the others departed, leaving only Rhys and Kelly.

I waved again, unsure if he could see me until he removed his wide-brimmed cap and waved.

Tears rolled down my cheeks as the airship lifted into the clouds, the castle falling out of sight.

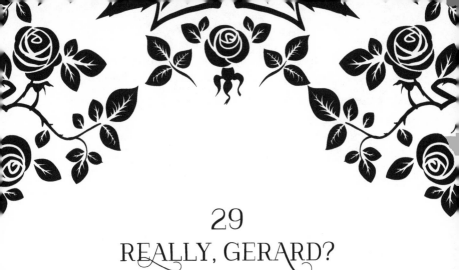

29
REALLY, GERARD?

I sat weeping miserably, my head on my arms.

"Isabelle? What is it?" Papa asked, sitting down beside me. "Are you sick, my girl?"

"No, Papa."

"Then what is it?"

"I'm just…sad."

My father took my hand. "Don't worry about anything. We'll take you directly home. I'll have Doctor Murray come at once. My poor, brave girl. Lord knows what you endured. It's all over now. It's all over," Papa said, pulling me into an embrace.

I didn't have it in me to tell him that it was far from over.

Papa kissed me on the forehead then left me to my thoughts.

The airship raced along. I breathed in the clean air. It felt good to be amongst the clouds, to feel the wind on my cheeks. It eased the sorrow that wracked my heart and helped me clear my mind. It wasn't a forever goodbye. All I had to do was make the key and go back.

I pulled out the small slip of paper, the imprint, and looked at it. It would take no time to make a windup key. I just needed a few days at the most. No more than a week. I slid my finger along the lines on the paper, the grooves of the key. For some reason, they seemed oddly familiar. I stared at the paper. The irony was not lost on me: I needed the key to his heart. I was sure that there had never before been a case quite so literal.

"Your father told me what you did for him, about your bravery. You are an impressive woman, Isabelle Hawking," Gerard said, taking a seat beside me.

"There is nothing I wouldn't sacrifice for Papa," I said, looking out into the misty white clouds.

Gerard nodded. "Admirable. I am sure you will make an equally devoted wife."

"Gerard," I said, seeking to stop him before he even began his usual devotions.

Gerard lifted a hand. "Please, Isabelle, hear me out. I know you think I am too flirtatious. I am. I have been. But I must confess, the other flirtations were always only for sport. With you, I am quite sincere in my affections."

"As I'm sure you say to all the ladies."

"No," Gerard said passionately. "No. You have been through so much, and I know you are not well, but when you recover, I hope you will give me the chance to show you how sincere I am. Please, allow me to prove to you that I am serious."

"But Gerard—"

"Isabelle, please. Do you not see?" he asked, motioning to the airship around him. "I have been working with your father night and day to find that strange island. I went through every map. Every archive. Talked to every scholar I knew. To find you."

I paused. That, at the least, was true. It was the most genuine act I'd ever seen from him.

"I am very grateful for your efforts, for helping Papa."

Gerard smiled. "It was my pleasure. I admire him greatly," he said. "And I esteem you more."

Taking me entirely by surprise, he reached out and grabbed my hand.

At the same moment, a sharp wind blew. The gust, coming from the island, blew so fiercely that it shifted the airship off course.

The crew and captain worked quickly to steady the ship.

But worse.

Even worse.

The moment Gerard thrust his hand into mine, the thin piece of paper I was holding—the tiny note that was the key to everything I needed—was wrenched from my grasp.

Gasping, I leaped up and desperately clawed at the wind in an effort to retrieve it.

The gust blew hard, and on it, I heard menacing laughter.

"No! Oh no," I yelled, jumping to grab the paper.

But the wind snatched it and ripped it away. It fluttered over the side of the ship and disappeared amongst the clouds.

30
154

There was a soft knock on the workshop door. I ignored it. My magnifying glass in front of me, I filed the last grove on the windup key.

"Isabelle?" Papa called.

I almost had it. I filed down the last slanted groove then set the key in the box with the others. I sat back in my seat and pushed my goggles onto my forehead.

"Isabelle?"

I huffed an exasperated sigh. "Yes? What is it?"

"Doctor Murray is here."

I frowned then pulled another template key from the box sitting on my desk. Inside the carton were a hundred like it, dummy keys not yet shaped or filed. I opened my journal and looked over my notes. I grabbed a pen, drew a line, and made a new remark: *Configuration 154.*

"Isabelle?"

"Yes. Yes. Send him in."

I pulled off my goggles and tossed them onto the table. I rose quickly, my back against my workbench.

"Ah, here is my patient," Doctor Murray said. "Hard at work, I see. A new sculpture, perhaps?"

My father looked from me to Doctor Murray, a worried expression on his face.

I slid a little to the left to hide my journal and the box of keys sitting there. "Oh, just tinkering," I said dismissively, forcing a smile.

Doctor Murray gave me a slight nod. "Master Hawking, will you give us just a moment?"

"Of course. I'll be in the parlor," Papa said then left.

"Miss Hawking, why don't you sit? I'm just here for a follow-up. I wanted to give you a quick examination, make sure you are still recovering well."

I sat but said nothing. He needed to hurry up. I didn't have time for this.

Doctor Murray dug through his bag. "How are you feeling? Any more headaches?"

"In the morning, yes. They pass by the afternoon."

"Are you eating breakfast? Some people experience weakness in the morning after a long fast."

"I... No, not with regularity. You're right. That's probably the culprit. I'll pay special attention to that starting tomorrow."

"What has you so busy first thing in the morning?" Doctor Murray asked.

I eyed the keys out of the corner or my eye but didn't answer.

Doctor Murray studied me closely. "Well, may I have a look?" he asked, motioning to the bandage. The cut on my forehead had required stitches. Doctor Murray, who had come to see me the day we'd come back, now almost a month ago, had done the job.

"Go ahead," I said.

Anything to get this over with and get back to my task.

Doctor Murray removed the bandage and inspected the

wound. Dipping into his doctor's bag, he pulled out some cleaning salves. I winced when he applied some alcohol. He then smeared a healing balm on the wound.

"It's coming along well. We were not in time to avoid a scar, I'm afraid," he said as he began to bandage the cut with a fresh dressing.

I don't care. What does a scar matter?

Doctor Murray paused, waiting for a reply, but I had nothing to say. It was a scar, a small blemish. It was nothing. What mattered was Rhys. Rhys was dying. I needed to work quickly. And right now, Doctor Murray was in my way.

I sat perfectly still, waiting for him to finish the job.

"So, your work," he said, looking at my bench as he packed up his tools and ointments. "Your father tells me you've been making keys."

"Papa should not gossip," I snapped.

Doctor Murray stiffened but said nothing. He removed a small device from his bag. "I would like to examine your eyes if that's all right."

"Fine."

Doctor Murray slid out a stool and sat down directly in front of me. He activated his small tool. Light glowed from the end of it. "Try not to blink," he said then shone the light directly into my eyes.

With key one hundred fifty-four, I'll try a variation on the one hundred thirty series. The second set of grooves might have slashed left then right as opposed to right then left. I could make a series varying the—

"How are you sleeping these days?"

"Fine."

—angle. I should have another series of ten done by the end of the day Friday. After that, I could begin a variation on the last set of slashes. Once those are done, I could—

"Your father tells me you sleep very little, and when you do sleep, you have bad dreams."

"Really, Doctor Murray, I am fine. I'm just busy."

"Miss Hawking, you had two blows to the head in a very short span of time. A single concussion is already a lot for the body to recover from. A second blow—"

"I said I'm fine," I replied hotly, turning away. A wave of embarrassment washed over me. I hadn't meant to be rude. I just…I just needed to hurry. And Doctor Murray really needed to leave. "I'm sorry, Doctor. I'm…distracted."

"You are not yet recovered, Miss Hawking. It would be better if you rested. This work can wait."

No. It can't.

I said nothing.

Doctor Murray rose and put his device away. "Miss Hawking, sometimes when a person experiences trauma, it can have an effect on their mind. Your father and I are concerned that what you experienced on that island has—"

"Doctor Murray," I said, standing. "I appreciate your concern. I will be sure to eat breakfast and get more rest, but I am not out of my wits, thank you very much. No need to secure me a cell in the sanatorium just yet."

"Isabelle," Doctor Murray said aghast. He then coughed uncomfortably. "Miss Hawking, I am not just your doctor. I am your friend. If you want to talk about what happened, I am here to listen. Or maybe you would prefer to talk to Elyse? I know sometimes there are things that are best discussed amongst women."

Oh good God. "No. No, thank you. I'll be fine. As you said, I am still recovering. I think I'm just trying to find my footing again, and I'm failing at the moment. It will all come together in time."

Doctor Murray lowered his chin into his cravat as he considered my words, a move I used to find terribly fetching. Now I just wanted him to leave.

"Very well. I'll call again on you Friday evening," he said.

"Good. Thank you."

We both stood there a moment until Doctor Murray said, "I'll show myself out."

I nodded to him then waited as he turned and left. When I heard the door close once more, I sat back down at my workbench. I slid my journal toward me, flipping back to the earlier 130 series, and began making a sketch of the next design.

I could hear Doctor Murray and Papa talking in the foyer. I rolled my eyes, feeling relieved when the front door finally opened and closed, heralding Doctor Murray's departure. When the sketch was finished, I grabbed the dummy windup key, a pair of tin snips, and a file, and began my work.

One hundred fifty-four.

31
WE HAVE TO GO BACK

It was late that night when I finally went upstairs and lay down on my bed. There was a tray with a plate of biscuits sitting on my side table, but the thought of food turned my stomach. I rolled over and stared at the ceiling.

There was a knock on the door.

"Isabelle?" Papa called.

"Yes?"

"It's Wednesday. I brought you some books from Mister Denick."

"Okay."

"May I come in?"

"Yes."

The door opened. "Oh, it's dark in here. I didn't know you were sleeping."

"I'm not."

Papa struck a match and lit a candle. "You're still dressed."

"Yes."

"Shall I set out a night dress for you?"

"No, thank you."

"Mister Denick sent you three volumes. I told him you'd taken an interest in Celtic lore. He had a good number of books on the topic. Apparently, there is a scholar by the name of S. Rossetti who has written an entire booklet on Ogham."

"Thank you, Papa. Please set them on the desk."

"Very well. Do you need anything, my dear?"

"No."

"Isabelle?"

"Yes, Papa?"

My father exhaled deeply. "Never mind. Goodnight, my dear."

"Goodnight."

My father left.

I lay there for a long time staring up at the canopy of my bed. The street outside our workshop was busy. Horse-drawn wagons rolled down the cobblestone street. I heard the roar of a steam-powered vehicle somewhere in the distance. Then there was the purr of airships gliding overhead. All the sounds of home. It should have comforted me, but...

I sat up and picked through the books sitting on the table. One volume was on illuminated Irish manuscripts. Yes, there would be details therein on the knotwork I'd seen. Another volume was a guide to the menhir in England. Disinterested, I set it aside. I picked up the last book, a small, leather-bound journal. With a tired sigh, I opened the book and flipped through the pages. Whomever the author was, they had developed a partial key to Ogham.

Thumbing from back to front, I flipped the pages over and over again. The pages turned quickly, moving before my glassy eyes like a phantasmagoria.

Flip.

Flip.

Flip.

The Ogham lines moved and shifted shapes.

Flip.

Flip.

I was about to flip through the journal again then I paused.

Rather than holding the book with the spine to the left, I turned the spine toward the top and flipped the pages once more.

When I did so, I gasped.

Tossing the book aside, I rushed to my table and pushed aside all my papers until I found the rubbing I had done of the Ogham mark on the stone on the Isle of Annwfn. I then grabbed my journal and turned to the pages where I'd noted the Ogham symbols.

"Oh my God," I whispered, my hands shaking. "Oh my God."

The Ogham symbols were typically read vertically. Down a single line was a series of slashes that signified letters or phrases. But when turned to the side...

Collecting all my things, the little leather book, and my satchel, I raced back downstairs to my workshop.

I spotted Papa sitting in the parlor reading and puffing on his pipe as I rushed past.

"Isabelle, is everything all right?"

"Yes... Finally, yes," I yelled then raced to my workshop, slamming the door closed behind me. I dumped all my items on my workbench, wincing when I heard a thud. I had forgotten Elyse's mirror was still inside.

Setting out all my papers, I looked at the repeating pattern. I then thumbed through the pages of my journal. After I'd lost the slip of paper—let it suffice to say that at that moment, any hope Gerard had of marrying me quickly faded as I called him every colorful name I knew, so much so that the airship crew paled—I'd written down the imprint as I remembered it. My first sketch, I thought, was exact, but in the days that followed, I doubted myself. There was no way I would return to the island without a key that would work. Therefore, I'd been working, making configurations based on the first design. I wanted to have every possible configuration ready just in case. I'd leave nothing else to chance. Nothing. Precision. Detail. Making sure I considered every shape, that was what would save Rhys. Not instinct.

But when I looked at the sketch of the first key I'd drawn, the one I'd noted down from memory, I realized I'd been wrong. I should have listened to my instincts.

I sat my sketch of the windup key alongside the Ogham symbols that had been on the standing stones.

They were a perfect match.

I rose and went to the box where I'd stored the windup keys. I dug through the box until I found the key tagged number 1. I inspected it against my notes and sketches. They were the same.

A soft hand settled on my shoulder.

I shrieked and jumped, knocking over the stool.

"Isabelle," Papa said carefully. "My daughter, I am so very concerned about you. I spoke to Doctor Murray and—"

I lifted the key. "Look," I said, motioning from the key to the sketches. "I've been trying to make this key. All this time, I've been trying to make sure I got it just right. I had to make sure I had the exact configuration. I had an imprint of the original keyhole, but I lost it to the wind. Gerard," I said, shaking my head with angry frustration. "But I have it now. I have the key. You see! I have it now. We have to go back."

"Isabelle, what are you saying?"

I stared at Papa. After losing the blueprint for the key due to Gerard's clumsy show of affection, I had not been able to think straight. I hadn't found a way to tell Papa about Rhys. I couldn't find the words. But now, I needed to go back, and I needed Papa's help.

"Papa, listen to me," I said. As I spoke, I grabbed a leather band from my workbench and tied it to the windup key which I then strung around my neck. "Please listen and try to understand. The automatons on the island are cursed. They were cursed by a fey creature. I saw her with my own eyes. The lord —Lord Rhys Llewellyn. The automaton is the real lord, the real man. Papa, do you understand me? That mech is a man. All the mechanicals there are people who've been cursed. Rhys was turned into an automaton by the faerie. This key. This key will keep him alive. I need to go back. I need to go back. I need to take him the key. I need to tell him I love him. Maybe if he knows, maybe he'll love me too, and the curse can be broken."

A tear streamed down Papa's cheek. "My daughter has gone mad," he whispered. "Oh Isabelle, what happened to you?"

"No, Papa," I said, taking him by the arms. "There are more things in this world than mortals like us can ever dream of. The island was a holy sanctuary for the Druids of old. Consider how close it is to Angelesy. The druids lived there and protected the first inhabitants of that island, the fey. You must believe me. I saw the faerie woman. She is the one who cursed them. How else can you explain how advanced those mechanicals are? No tinker alive has ever created anything like them. They are not machines. They are people, cursed people. They need our help! I have the key now. I must go back."

"Isabelle, you are raving. What you're talking about sounds like fairy tales."

Fairy tales.

Fairy tales.

Elyse's mirror!

I turned and opened my satchel, pulling out the mirror. Grabbing Papa by the arm, I turned off the lantern that had been burning in my workshop and led Papa to the window. It was cloudy outside. Rain was coming. But there was still just enough moonlight. This had to work, or I was going to wake up tomorrow morning at Carfax Sanatorium.

"What is this? Is this the mirror Elyse gave you?"

"Fairy tales," I said with a nod to Papa. "Now watch. Mirror, show me Rhys."

At first, there was nothing.

"Isabelle, I think we should—"

The handle and frame began to glow blue.

"What is this?" Papa whispered.

The image was smoky at first, but soon cleared. When it did so, I began to see the shapes of the bedchamber in which I had slept at the castle. The images were fuzzy at first, but I saw Missus Silver and Mister Flint standing beside the bed. On the bed, I spotted Kelly. Was she ill? What was wrong?

As the image shifted and cleared, I saw with horror that it was Rhys lying on the bed.

Missus Silver stood weeping at the bedside.

Rhys's optics had grown very dim. He held Mister Flint's hand. I could not make out their words, but I didn't need to. It was clear what was happening. Rhys was dying.

"I need to go. Now. We need to go. Now," I said, turning to Papa.

Outside, thunder rolled and lightning struck somewhere far off.

"Isabelle," Papa said, looking wide-eyed at me. "Is it true?"

"It is. It is, Papa. They are all mortal. But they are cursed. I know how to save him, but I must get there before it's too late."

"But he—"

"I must go to him, Papa. I must go. Now."

Papa nodded. "Very well. Let me collect the map LeBoeuf prepared and get my coat. Will you need all of these?" he said, motioning to the other keys I had created.

I looked down at the single key hanging on my chest, the perfect match to the Ogham writing.

"No. This one will be enough."

"Are you sure?"

It was a leap of faith. "Yes."

"Very good. Get ready then, my girl. We'll head to the airship towers at once."

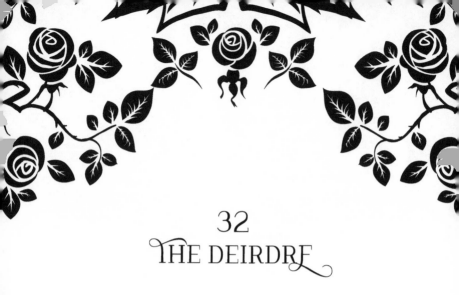

32
THE DEIRDRE

By the time we reached the airship towers, the rainstorm had turned violent. Wind whipped, lightning cracked, and thunder rolled across the horizon. I glared at the sky. If the fey woman wanted to stop me, she'd have to drown me this time.

Fighting against the wind and rain, we rushed to the tower lift that would take us to the airships docked above.

"No one up there," the tower guard said. "Weather is too bad. All the ships are grounded."

"Where are all the pilots?" Papa asked.

"Over at the Hopper," the guard said, pointing to a tavern nearby called Rose's Hopper. The place was a popular watering hole for airship jockeys.

"Let's go," I said to Papa, motioning in the direction of the pub.

"Good luck. Only a fool would go out in this weather," the tower guard said then headed back into the guard station.

I frowned at the man, then Papa and I headed quickly to the tavern. Inside, the pub was packed. Airship jockeys drank, sang, fought, and jostled each other as they stood almost arm to arm in the crowded bar.

"I'll ask the tapper," Papa said then headed toward the bar.

I stood by the door eyeing over the pilots. My assessment of them at the market was right. Three-fourths of them were nothing more than scoundrels. Many of them were already passed out drunk at their tables.

"Oi, any of you lot willing to take a flight to Wales?" the tapper called.

The room silenced for a moment then the rowdy crowd started laughing.

I scanned the tavern, my eyes trying to meet those of anyone who might be willing, anyone whom I could convince to help me for all the coin in my dowry.

"My dear, we'll have to wait until the storm passes," Papa said.

My eyes welled with tears. "But Papa."

"Isabelle, this weather is too severe. These men won't risk their lives for us."

"Surely someone will take the job. Papa, please, I don't care the cost. You saw... We must hurry!"

Papa pulled me close to him and kissed the top of my head. "We'll make it in time. We'll still make it in time."

I wiped a tear from my cheek and looked across the tavern to see a young girl, maybe no more than fourteen or fifteen years old, give me a hard look. She then whispered into the ear of her kilt-wearing companion. They both glanced at the elderly man passed out at the table beside them, then with a nod to one another, they slid out of the booth and made their way to Papa and me.

"Hear you're looking for a ship," the young man said, his Scottish accent thick.

"Yes. We know the weather is dreadful, but it's an emergency. We must get to Wales tonight."

"It'll be a bumpy ride," the Scotsman said.

Hope flowered in my chest. "It doesn't matter."

"And it won't be cheap," he added.

"We will pay you for the trouble," Papa told him. "We're just grateful to find a pilot willing to take us."

The man laughed. "I'm not the pilot. She is."

We turned and looked at the girl. She was a pretty thing with brown hair, big eyes, and an expression that was far too hard for someone her age.

"Oh. Very well. I'm willing to pay—" Papa began then leaned in close to the pair.

The pilot nodded to her Scottish companion.

"We're in. I'm Angus," the young man said, sticking out his hand, which Papa and I both shook. "That's Lily."

Lily nodded to us.

"Right, then. Come on," the young man said as he pulled on his coat, the girl doing the same. The two of them headed outside.

Papa and I exchanged a glance then followed them. They were a cagey pair, but there was a certainty in the girl's walk and expression that I knew and understood. She was not going to have any trouble flying in this storm. The storm, on the other hand, didn't dare get in her way.

As we approached the airship tower lift, the same guard appeared.

"Lily, are you out of your mind?" the guard said.

"What? It's just a little rain," she replied with a smirk, holding out her hand as if the torrent were nothing.

The guard shook his head. "She's going to get you killed, Angus."

The Scotsman laughed. "Lily could outrun Zeus's lightning bolts."

"Where's Fletcher? He'll be none too pleased to discover you've slunk off," the guard said.

"Passed out drunk at the Hopper. We'll be back before he wakes up," Lily replied.

The guard nodded then opened the lift for us to go up.

Once we were inside, the girl operated the crank, and we headed up.

The higher we got, the windier it was. It was raining in heavy sheets, the wind whipping violently.

The lift stopped on the third platform. Once we were all out, Lily reached back inside the compartment and sent the lift back down. She turned, and we headed down the airship platform behind her.

"Here's the *Deirdre*," Angus said, motioning for Papa and me to follow them aboard the ship. The pilot had already boarded and was climbing up to the burner basket. "You'd do best to head into the captain's quarters."

The ship rocked in her berth. All around, I heard the jingling of rigging.

"Can you get the burner lit, Lil?" Angus called up.

"Yeah, she'll come," the girl replied. A moment later, we saw the glow of orange as the balloon started to fill with hot air.

Angus began unleashing the anchor lines.

Papa motioned for me to follow him into the captain's cabin. It was a small space, filled with maps, equipment, and a small bench. Staring ahead absently, I sat down while Papa pulled out the map Gerard had made.

We're going to make it on time.

We'll make it on time.

The door opened and Lily entered. "Where are we heading?" she asked as she slipped on a pair of gloves.

"Here," Papa said, showing her the map.

"An island?"

"Yes, we must get there as quickly as possible. It's an emergency."

She looked over the map, setting the coordinates on her modified compass, then turned to go, but she paused first and looked back at me. She studied my face closely then said, "Don't worry, miss. I'll get you there in no time." She smiled softly then closed the door behind her.

A few moments later, I felt the airship lift out of her berth then turn west.

Fighting to be heard over the wind, Lily shouted directives to Angus as the ship continued to rise.

The airship rose up.

And up.

And up.

And up.

And up.

"Papa," I said, feeling suddenly worried.

Papa, who also looked confused, headed outside. I went to the door of the captain's cabin and looked out. My senses were right. We were rising…quickly.

"Trying to get above the rain," Lily called. "There," she said, pointing to an opening between two storm clouds. "Up and out."

"Like the clashing rocks in Jason and the Argonauts," Papa said.

The pilot laughed then yanked on the bell to the gear galley. "Angus, ease ten percent."

Papa looked to the pilot and up again. "You'll need more lift to get up and out."

"Yes, I know," the pilot called.

"And you'll have to reduce your lift when you break through the cloud bank, or the air temperature will send us shooting up to the heavens."

"Is that right?

"Yes, it is. I can man the balloon," Papa shouted over the wind.

"Sir, I beg your pardon, but maybe it's better if you go back inside."

"My dear, I am Master Arthur Hawking. I can man your balloon burner. I am the one who designed it, after all."

At that, the girl laughed. "Then be my guest, Master Hawking."

Papa looked back at me. I nodded to him then braced myself against the doorframe. Lightning struck all around us as we quickly lifted up between the storm clouds.

The young pilot watched everything. The sky, the balloon, the ship, the lightning strikes, the wind. Impressed, I observed her as she made her careful ascent.

Lightning crashed so close to us that it hurt my eyes.

"Master Hawking, increase the burn another five percent," Lily called to Papa.

My hands shook seeing him riding in the balloon basket. This was my papa as I'd never seen him before, my papa as he'd been when he was young. He and mother had lived the early years of their marriage more frequently aloft than on the ground.

The wind whipped hard.

Isabelle. Isabelle.

"I'm coming for him whether you like it or not," I whispered.

Laughter rippled across the sky, buried in a crack of lightning, which struck beside us.

The sound was deafening.

My ears rang.

The light burned my eyes.

The pilot, however, had seemed to sense the bolt coming and turned the ship quickly, avoiding getting struck.

"Jesus Christ," Angus yelled from below deck. The door to the gear galley flapped open. "Lily, we hit?"

"No. Close though," she said then turned the ship, aligning it with the break in the clouds.

"Master Hawking, twenty percent more heat. Now. Angus, stop the rudder."

Angus disappeared below deck as Papa turned the dials and levers. Bright orange flame shot upward, the ship rising fast.

Up.

Up.

Up and through the slim gap between the clouds, which had been a moving target all the while. The *Deirdre* slipped right between the two banks of storm clouds just as the pilot had planned.

A moment later, we were moving above two towers of storm clouds. The sky overhead was full of stars, the moon shining brightly.

Papa adjusted the heat on the balloon. Hot air slipped out of a valve flap at the very top. The airship's lift slowed.

"Now, Angus. Full ahead," Lily called.

The rudder on the back of the ship began turning quickly, and the ship shot off to the west. Lily checked her compass once more, made a slight adjustment, then leaned back, smirking contentedly.

I smiled at her, my grin reaching from ear to ear. I stepped away from the doorframe and stared up at the moon and stars. The air was so pure, so fresh. It felt magical.

"It's beautiful," I said, looking back at the gifted young pilot.

"That it is," she agreed.

"Thank you, Lily."

She inclined her head to me.

Turning, I went to the prow of the ship and gazed out at the horizon.

"Hold on, Rhys. I'm coming for you."

33
THE KEY TO MY HEART

THE AIRSHIP *DEIRDRE* DESCENDED OVER THE ISLAND JUST AS the first light of dawn turned the dark night's sky pale gray. Soft yellow light trimmed the horizon. My heart beat hard as I wrapped my hand around the windup key. As soon as we were low over the garden, Lily steadied the ship. Angus emerged from below and threw the rope ladder overboard.

"Papa," I called, barely holding myself from leaping to the ground.

"Go, Isabelle. I'll be just behind you."

I went to the side of the ship.

Lily extended her hand, helping me slip around the side of the ship and onto the ladder.

"Thank you," I told her.

She nodded at me. "Good luck, Miss Hawking."

I descended the ladder quickly. When I reached the ground, I raced across the garden just as Mister Flint opened the front door.

Tears of oil soiled his face. "Miss Hawking," he said sadly.

"Am I too late? Is he still alive?"

"Barely. Oh, Miss Hawking. We had nearly given up hope."

I raced past him and back to the castle. I rushed up the steps, taking the stairs two at a time, to the chamber. Not waiting, I burst in.

Missus Silver, who had been sitting at the side of the bed, rose abruptly, startled by the sudden intrusion.

"Isabelle!" she said.

I rushed to Rhys's bedside.

"Rhys. Rhys," I said, scooping up his hand. The lights inside his optics were dim. Only the faintest flicker remained. I lay my ear against his chest. Inside, I heard a slow tick no stronger than water dripping from a leaking pump.

The door clicked shut behind me as Missus Silver left us alone.

"Rhys? Rhys, can you hear me?" I called, touching his cheek. To my shock, he felt like cold metal. "Rhys?"

His optics flicked toward me and tried to focus, but there was no use. The light within was almost out. He opened his mouth to speak, but no sound came out. He lifted his hand just slightly, but it dropped onto the bed.

"No, no, no, no, no," I said, quickly unbuttoning his shirt. I yanked the key from around my neck, kissed it for luck, then slowly slipped it into his chest. The key fit perfectly. I felt the grooves align. Taking a deep breath, I turned the windup key. I wound the key over and over, my eyes going from Rhys's face back to the key again. He should be reanimating by now. The lights in his optics should be coming back to life.

I wound and wound until I could wind no further.

I looked from the key to Rhys once more.

The lights in his optics had gone out.

"Rhys?" I whispered.

Slowly, I began to pull out the key. As with the others, this should reactivate him.

"Rhys?"

Holding my breath, I pulled the key out all the way.

There was nothing.

Nothing.

No light.

No movement.

No anything.

"Rhys? Rhys?" I said, setting my ear against his chest.

Nothing.

He'd become still, cold, and silent.

"No. No, no, no. I made it in time. This isn't fair! I made it in time," I yelled, knowing the fey woman could hear me.

"Rhys," I said, gently holding his face in my hands. Tears streamed down my cheeks. He was… He was just gone. He was nothing more than a piece of metal. "Oh God, no. No. No. Oh God, no," I whispered, pressing my face against his, feeling the cold sensation of metal when our cheeks met.

"Rhys," I whispered. "Rhys, I'm so sorry. I'm so, so sorry. I love you. I love you. This can't be happening. I love you, you beastly machine. Do you hear me? I love you," I whispered.

Wind blew in from the open window with such strength that it made all the curtains hanging around the poster bed flutter. The air felt tingly, and I smelled the soft scents of flowers and earth.

I looked up to see the fey woman standing there, her blue robes flying all around her. She floated above the ground in a halo of glimmering gold.

She looked at me, my face wet with tears, then at Rhys.

She smiled softly at me then set her hand on Rhys's heart. His metal body came alive with golden light. The light became so bright that I closed my eyes, turning away to shield myself from the light. The wind whipped wildly around me.

And then, it stopped.

The first rays of the sun shone over the horizon, filling the room with rosy light.

I turned from the window back to Rhys to find a real,

living, breathing, man lying there. His eyes were the same silver color I'd seen on the boy in the painting. He had a mop of curly black hair and a well-trimmed pickdevant beard.

"Rhys?" I whispered.

Reaching up slowly, tepidly, he touched my cheek.

He winced then, closing his eyes as he gently stroked my skin with his fingertips.

I took his hand into mine.

"Rhys," I whispered. "I love you."

He sat up slowly. Moving carefully, he touched my hair. He looked deeply into my eyes. "I love you too," he whispered then leaned in and kissed me.

And when I felt the press of his flesh against my lips, I knew the curse was broken.

34
HAPPILY EVER AFTER, OF COURSE

"My lord! My lord!" I heard Missus Silver call from the hallway.

In her excitement, she threw open the door and raced into the room.

Rhys drew back, pausing to touch my chin gently, staring into my eyes.

"Lord Rhys. Miss Hawking. Look!"

I turned and looked back to find Missus Silver, the real Missus Silver, standing there. She had a sweet face lined with wrinkles. Her hair, a mix of black and silver, was pulled back in a bun, and her eyes were a soft blue color.

"Missus Silver," I said, rising.

The woman pulled me into her arms. "Oh, Miss Hawking, I just knew you were the one," she whispered into my ear.

"Mama," another voice called. A moment later, a red-haired woman who was about my age appeared at the door.

"Bronwyn? Bronwyn!" Missus Silver let me go and raced across the room to embrace her daughter.

From the foyer below, I heard the sound of loud cheers and singing.

A bark sounded in the hallway, and a moment later, a very real Kelly raced into the room, jumping on the bed with Rhys.

"Kelly," he said, patting her ears. He set his forehead on hers.

I reached out for Rhys who rose, and we all went to the hall. In the main foyer, Mister Flint, Missus Smith, and Mister Steele were dancing a jig. When they saw Rhys, they raced toward him and grabbed ahold of him, Missus Silver and Bronwyn joining in the embrace.

Kelly ran out the front door, through which I spied Papa.

Leaving the others for a moment, I stepped outside with my father.

"Look," Papa said, motioning in front of him.

We watched as the metal retreated from the castle, the flowers and bushes returning to green once more. The metal faded as it reached the wall, and once more, the garden was alive. A silvery blue butterfly flew by, landing on a red rose.

I looked up at the sky which was clear and bright. Pink, orange, and yellow hues lit up the skyline. I watched as the *Deirdre* rose up into the clouds and disappeared.

Barking happily, Kelly raced around the garden chasing every smell and sound.

I felt someone approach from behind and turned to find Rhys there. He took my hand in his and stared down at me, gently stroking my cheek once more.

"Master Hawking, I must beg your forgiveness for my rudeness," Rhys said, never taking his eyes from me.

Papa coughed. Twice. "You are quite forgiven, Lord Llewellyn."

"And I must ask your forgiveness a second time."

"For what?"

"For taking your daughter from you," he said then knelt before me. "Isabelle Hawking, be my wife," he said, pressing something into my hand.

I looked down to see it was the windup key.

"Only you have the key to my heart," Rhys added.

Papa chuckled good-naturedly and set his hand on Rhys's shoulder.

"Isabelle, you didn't answer," Papa said.

I laughed out loud. "Yes. Of course. With all my heart. Yes."

The wind blew softly once more, and from the depths of the forest, I heard a voice on the breeze: *Isabelle, welcome home.*

EPILOGUE

"WHAT DO YOU THINK?" RHYS ASKED.

I lowered the book I was reading and looked up at the canvas sitting on the easel. I smiled.

"You've captured her perfectly," I said. Rhys had been painting a picture of Kelly, who'd been playing in the brook near the hermitage all morning. The portrait depicted Kelly standing knee-deep in the pool amongst the lily pads. On a branch loaded with pink dogwood blossoms hanging just above the pool of water was Matilda. A glimmering beam of sunlight illuminated the sweet songbird's yellow feathers.

He set his paintbrush in a jar then came and looked over my shoulder. "And you, my love, what have you discovered?"

My journal lay open on my lap. It had taken a few weeks, but I was finally done. I tapped my pen on my pad. "I think I have it," I said, pointing to the line of Ogham and its translation in the notebook. With the booklet on Ogham Papa had brought me from the Hungerford Market, and a lot of study, I had successfully translated the line of Ogham writing that had been engraved on Rhys's key.

"And what did the key to my heart say?" Rhys asked.

I gazed up at him. "Love looks not with the eyes but with the mind."

Rhys furrowed his brow. "Isn't that a Shakespeare quote? But that's not possible. Ogham is ancient."

I smiled. "It was Shakespeare who was quoting."

Rhys smiled then stroked a stray hair away from my face. "My beauty," he whispered.

"My beastly," I replied, pinching his cheek, making him chuckle.

Leaning in, he set the softest of kisses on my lips.

And it was everything I ever dreamed of.

AUTHOR'S NOTE

I hope you enjoyed this steampunk twist on the classic *Beauty and the Beast* tale. I had a ton of fun reading the many different versions of the classic fairy tale in preparation for writing my own *Beauty and the Beast* book. Of course, I think we all know the Disney classic which I played on just a bit here. The original tale has a lot of similarities to Cinderella and offered a wide range of Beauties, Beasts, and a cast of evil sisters and loathsome brothers for Beauty. I loved the idea that Beauty's father was a merchant, and refashioning him as a tinker was a delight. But one thing I have always hated about *Beauty and the Beast* is the Stockholm Syndrome element. Beast's behavior is often abusive or borderline abusive. No one needs to encourage women to fall in love with their abusers. I hoped to cast that dynamic in a new light here. What I most enjoyed about writing this retelling was placing Isabelle and her father in a steampunk environment. I think the pair fits nicely in my steampunk universe. Belle is my favorite Disney princess because she is the intellectual. I wanted to keep that quality but mold it. I hope you enjoyed my twist on her character.

If you have read *Ice and Embers: Steampunk Snow Queen*, you already got a look at Isabelle and her papa through the eyes of Elyse McKenna (Murray). I enjoyed rewriting the scene at the dock from Isabelle's perspective. We leave *Ice and Embers* feeling happy for Elyse and Kai and their HEA. But what about Isabelle? How did she feel about losing a potential beau? It was fun to consider. If you'd like a closer look at Elyse and Doctor Kai Murray, please check out *Ice and Embers: Steampunk Snow Queen*.

I hope my fans of the *Airship Racing Chronicles* series enjoyed the cameo of a young Lily and Angus. I LOVED writing the scene on the *Deirdre*. It was like spending time with old friends. *The Airship Racing Chronicles* is my first steampunk series. It is definitely an adult series (sex, drugs, and airships), but if you're interested in reading Lily and Angus's story, check out *Chasing the Star Garden*.

As for the other fun pieces in the book, fans of *Lost* might have noticed a few iconic lines from that series floating around this book. As a Lostie, I've always wanted to write a "lost island" book. I gave it a shot. Hey, it's a leap of faith, right?

I also really had fun writing Kelly, who is named and modeled after a dog I had as a child.

There are a few more Easter Eggs in here that will make sense as you read the entire *Steampunk Fairy Tales* series and *The Airship Racing Chronicles*. Both series are set in the same steampunk universe.

Thank you for taking the time to read *Beauty and Beastly*. I hope you enjoyed the novel.

ACKNOWLEDGMENTS

Many thanks to Becky Stephens for pulling my ass out of the fire…again. I couldn't do it without you!

Carrie Wells, thank you for all you do!

A special thanks to all my Steampunk Fairy Tales ARC readers!

Thank you to Karri Klawiter for designing such a beautiful cover.

As always, thank you to the BIC group, Erin Hayes, Margo Bond Collins, Jessica Nelson, and my beloved family for all of your support.

ABOUT THE AUTHOR

Melanie Karsak is the author of *The Airship Racing Chronicles*, *The Harvesting Series*, *The Burnt Earth Series*, *The Celtic Blood Series*, and the *Steampunk Fairy Tales Series*. A steampunk connoisseur, zombie whisperer, and heir to the iron throne, the author currently lives in Florida with her husband and two children. She is an Instructor of English at Eastern Florida State College.

KEEP IN TOUCH WITH MELANIE ONLINE

MelanieKarsak.com
Facebook.com/AuthorMelanieKarsak
Twitter.com/MelanieKarsak
Pinterest.com/MelanieKarsak

Check out all of Melanie's *Steampunk Fairy Tales*
Beauty and Beastly: Steampunk Beauty and the Beast
Ice and Embers: Steampunk Snow Queen
Curiouser and Curiouser: Steampunk Alice in Wonderland

Ready to go airship racing? Meet Lily and her crew in *The Airship Racing Chronicles* (this series contains mature content)
Chasing the Star Garden
Chasing the Green Fairy

JOIN MELANIE'S NEWSLETTER

http://eepurl.com/cM53pv

Made in the USA
Columbia, SC
29 July 2022

64050509R00126